5V

ACR 5506

SANTA CRUZ CITY-COUNTY LIBRARY SYSTEM
0000114785

D0437565

FICTION AUC

Auchincloss, Louis.

Manhattan monologues.

7/02

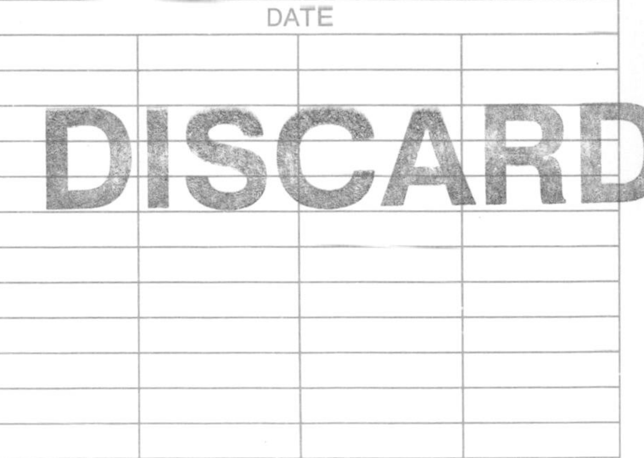

2/03-12

SANTA CRUZ PUBLIC LIBRARY
Santa Cruz, California

BAKER & TAYLOR

MANHATTAN MONOLOGUES

Also by Louis Auchincloss

FICTION

The Indifferent Children
The Injustice Collectors
Sybil
A Law for the Lion
The Romantic Egoists
The Great World and Timothy Colt
Venus in Sparta
Pursuit of the Prodigal
The House of Five Talents
Portrait in Brownstone
Powers of Attorney
The Rector of Justin
The Embezzler
Tales of Manhattan
A World of Profit
Second Chance
I Come as a Thief
The Partners
The Winthrop Covenant
The Dark Lady
The Country Cousin
The House of the Prophet
The Cat and the King
Watchfires
Narcissa and Other Fables
Exit Lady Masham
The Book Class
Honorable Men
Diary of a Yuppie

Skinny Island
The Golden Calves
Fellow Passengers
The Lady of Situations
False Gods
Three Lives
Tales of Yesteryear
The Collected Stories of Louis Auchincloss
The Education of Oscar Fairfax
The Atonement and Other Stories
The Anniversary and Other Stories
Her Infinite Variety

Nonfiction

Reflections of a Jacobite
Pioneers and Caretakers
Motiveless Malignity
Edith Wharton
Richelieu
A Writer's Capital
Reading Henry James
Life, Law and Letters
Persons of Consequence:
Queen Victoria and Her Circle
False Dawn: Women in the
Age of the Sun King
The Vanderbilt Era
Love Without Wings
The Style's the Man
La Glorie: The Roman Empire
of Corneille and Racine
The Man Behind the Book

Manhattan Monologues

LOUIS AUCHINCLOSS

Houghton Mifflin Company
BOSTON NEW YORK
2002

Copyright © 2002 by Louis Auchincloss

All rights reserved

For information about permission to reproduce selections from this book, write to Permissions, Houghton Mifflin Company, 215 Park Avenue South, New York, New York 10003.

Visit our Web site: www.houghtonmifflinbooks.com.

Library of Congress Cataloging-in-Publication Data

Auchincloss, Louis.
Manhattan monologues / Louis Auchincloss.
p. cm.
ISBN 0-618-15289-X
1. New York (N.Y.) — Social life and customs — Fiction.
2. Manhattan (New York, N.Y.) — Fiction. I. Title.
PS3501.U25 M36 2002
813'.54—dc21 2001051618

Book design by Anne Chalmers
Typefaces: Janson Text, Agfa Sackers Antique, Type Embellishments

Printed in the United States of America

QUM 10 9 8 7 6 5 4 3 2 1

To Andrew and Tracy

Contents

Old New York

Entre Deux Guerres

Nearer Today

Old New York

All That May Become a Man

I HAVE NEVER dropped the junior from my name, Ambrose Vollard, even after my father's death, because I always felt that the important thing about me was that I was his son. It was not that he was a distinguished historical figure—he wasn't. He lived the life, as my mother once put it, of a "charming idler," the adequately endowed New York gentleman of Knickerbocker forebears who had dedicated his existence to sport and adventure. But he was also a hero — that was the real point — to his non-heroic only son. As a Rough Rider he had charged up San Juan Hill after his beloved leader, the future President; he had slaughtered dozens of the most dangerous beasts of the globe; and he had attended expeditions to freezing and tropical uncharted lands for museums and zoos.

As a child I was obsessed with the notion that youth was only a preparation for the rigors of manhood. I was fourteen when the battleship *Maine* was blown up in the harbor of Havana, and I could never forget the noisy reaction of Father and his two brothers at the family board in Washington Square or their enthusiastic welcome of the prospect of war. They actually hoped to see New York under fire from the Spanish fleet, and America awakened from its slothful torpor and materialism by the clarion call to arms! The Vollard brothers were all tall bony men, with fine knobbly aristocratic features, who spoke in decibels higher than anyone else's, dominating every conversation with their loud mocking laughs, never guilty of any "business" but zestfully using the remnants of an old real estate fortune in pursuit of the fox, the grizzly bear or the lion, while not neglecting — for no Philistines they! — the reading of great books or the viewing of great pictures or even, if they could be silent long enough, the hearing of great music. I used to think of Father as a kind of amiable Cesare Borgia. I looked at him with an awe sandwiched between two dreads: the dread of never being able to emulate him and the dread of his finding this out.

Colonel Roosevelt, as he was always referred to in the family, even after he had received higher titles, was Father's god as well as friend. This great man, for all his multiple interests, had time in his life for men like the Vollards, whose zeal and courage and love of violent action made up, to his mind anyway, for their social inutility. I was introduced early, not only to the Colonel but to his books, and was indoctrinated in the creed that bravery was the sovereign virtue in a man, that a "splendid little war" like the Spanish one had been a blessing in disguise to preserve our national virility and that a coward was not a man at all.

And women? What of them? Well, their role was simpler: to inspire men and to bear children. Why, I sometimes agonized, in the deep, dark, deluding safety of the night, had I not been born a woman? And I knew, I always knew, that the mere presence of this evil wish, even in the innermost recesses of my mind, damned me forever. At least with men. Was there any hope of redemption in the eyes of women? Did Mother suspect what I was going through? I sometimes wondered.

Leonie Vollard was as small and white and quiet as her husband was big and brown and noisy, but she was in no way subservient. Despite their obvious deep devotion to each other, they nonetheless preserved inviolate their respective and distinctly separate "spheres of interest." She never protested against his long absences on hunting and exploratory expeditions, nor did he ever interfere with her exquisite housekeeping in the lovely red-brick early Federal house in Washington Square. She sat silently through the spirited, even raucous arguments of the Vollard clan at her dinner table, and he was a subdued guest at the readings of her poetry club. In his den he was allowed any number of animal trophies, but no claw, hoof, horn or antler was permitted in her chaste blue-and-yellow parlor. Similarly, the children were divided; my two younger sisters were left largely to their mother's care and supervision, while my guidance and training were Father's primary responsibilities. Yet Mother never conveyed any impression that she was unconcerned with my welfare. Quiet and reserved as she was, she managed to radiate the feeling that every unit of her family was equally important to her.

Certainly the thing that confused me most in my relationship with Father was that he was the most amiable, the most enchanting parent one could imagine. Of course, that had to be because he had no conception of what was going on inside me. His patient joviality in teaching me to ride, to jump, to shoot and to hunt, first the pheasant and then the fox, on our Long Island estate was never marred by reprehension of my ineptitudes, but loudly expressed by applause at my every successful effort. And in due time I learned to conduct myself with some competence in riding and shooting, aided by my earnest desire to accomplish the seemingly hopeless task of becoming the youth Father cheerfully insisted on believing I was. To follow his graceful figure across the fields after the hounds was indeed a pleasure, but I never lost sight of what to me were the inevitable future tests of manhood that I believed awaited me as the real justification for my training: that war where I would have to fight an enemy, perhaps hand to hand, in mud and horror, or the African safari where I would be obliged to stand rigid before a charging rhino.

At Saint Jude's, the boys' boarding school in Massachusetts to which I was sent, I was slightly more relaxed, relieved as I was, except on parents' weekends, of Father's pushing-me-on presence, although the academy heartily endorsed his athletic enthusiasms, including football, a game I particularly detested. Father went so far as to say that he would be ashamed of any son or nephew who didn't go in for the game. I was tall for my age but slender, and I got knocked about on the field quite painfully, yet I survived, and not too discreditably. Father, who came up to school frequently to view the Saturday afternoon games, was aware of my difficulty and did his best to reassure me. Walking back to the gymnasium after a match, he put an arm around my shoulders and said: "You mustn't mind, dear boy, if you don't make the school varsity team. A man can do just so much with the physique God has given him, and you've done everything that could be expected of a boy with your muscular equipment. I am very proud of you. In a couple of years you may become heftier, but it doesn't matter, because you'll always do the best with what you've got, and that's all that can be expected of any man."

Oh, yes, he made allowances; he always did for me. He was determined to squeeze me somehow into his male heaven.

But in the fall of my next-to-last year at the school I came close, for the first time in my life, to something faintly resembling an outer protest against Saint Jude's echo of Father's principles. This new little spurt of defiance was no doubt fostered by Father's absence, not only from the school but the country on an extended expedition to the Antarctic.

I began, at first surreptitiously, to skip the near compulsory attendance at the Saturday afternoon football matches between Saint Jude's and visiting teams. This was considered a serious breach of the required "school spirit," and when it became known that I had been caught in the library during our match with Chelton, the supreme athletic contest of the school year, I was shocked to find myself condemned to the humiliation of being "pumped."

This grave punishment of a graver offense consisted of being ordered to stand up before the whole school at roll call to be berated by the senior monitor (no faculty being present, as if to emphasize the *hors la loi* aspect of the proceeding) and then to be hustled by six sturdy members of the senior class down to the cellar to be half-drowned in the laundry wash basin.

The actual experience was soon over, but the shame was supposed to be deep and lasting. Yet I was oddly unmindful of the social ostracism that followed the event. It was something of a relief to be known at last for the poor thing I was. My only real concern was what Father would think. Would he even hear of it? I madly hoped not.

Of course he did, and from the headmaster himself in a special report to my parents. Home from the South Pole, he came right up to the school and took me for a Sunday afternoon walk through the woods to the river. It was a gloomy day, cold and cloudy, and I felt as bare as the stripped November trees. But the pain and concern on poor Father's face and the gentleness of his tone took me at last out of myself, and my mind turned over feverishly, seeking a way to spare his feelings.

"But what was your point, dear boy, in absenting yourself from the games? Was it to have more time to study?"

"Oh, no."

"Was it possibly to be alone to do something that was prohibited? Like smoking or drinking? You needn't be afraid that your old father will give you away. I'm just trying to understand; that's all."

And then I had it! It was a desperate try, but it was all I had. "I wanted to test my courage! I wanted to see if I could stand up to the worst thing that could happen to me in school! I *wanted* to be pumped!"

Of course, this was a bare-faced lie. I had had no notion that I would be caught or, if caught, that I would be so severely punished. But Father's face, though bewildered, was clearing, and I hurried on. "Boys my age haven't had the chance to prove themselves the way you did in the Spanish war! I wanted to see how I would stand up in a crisis. And I did! I did!"

Father had tears in his eyes as he turned to hug me. "Oh, my dear fellow, you went much too far! I'm afraid I've done too much bragging about my own tiny feats. What have I ever done but kill a few animals?"

"And men," I added stoutly.

"Well, we have to do that in war, regrettably. But, dear son, you must learn to moderate yourself. You have to live in this world, and that involves a certain amount of compromise.

Not of your honor, of course, but in small social matters such as attending popular events, even if they bore you. One mustn't let oneself get too prickly. And as for courage, dear boy, you have as much of it as any proud father could wish!"

My next real nervous crisis was delayed by four years. After my sophomore year at Harvard, Father took me along on what I had always regarded as the inevitable test—a hunting safari in Kenya. Mother and my sisters, of course, were left behind in the enviable security of New York; it was only I who had to be exposed to what Father gleefully assured me would be the thrill of my lifetime.

We set forth into the veldt with one of my uncles and a couple of enthusiastic young male cousins, a white hunter and some thirty bearers (the Vollard men always did things poshly). I had, reluctantly, to admit that I liked the countryside. It rolled away romantically and awesomely to the horizon on all sides, and had it been stripped of animal and insect life, I could have imagined enjoying myself. But of course it fairly teemed with both, and my relatives were intent on seeking the largest and most dangerous of the fauna. They soon found them.

The days were bad enough, with a charging elephant or Cape buffalo or lion brought down by Vollard fire two or three times a week, but the nights were worse. Our white hunter assured me that the great beasts that wandered through our camp at night would never break into a tent, but how could I be sure of that? Why would the mate of an elephant slaughtered in daylight not take revenge on its helpless murderers in the dark? I would toss on my cot for hours until sheer exhaustion robbed me of consciousness. And the huge bugs! Ugh!

Father noticed that I was tired, and sometimes he mercifully left me in camp to rest while the others were out shooting. But even then I would be nervous, left alone with a few unarmed bearers while animals prowled around and the guns were away. When I went out with them, Father usually kept me at his side, and he was noisily congratulatory when I shot and killed an oryx and then an eland. Neither of the poor beasts had tried to do anything but get away from us. And we were blessedly approaching the end of our terrible safari when the moment that I had dreaded burst upon me. Our hunter had spotted a huge old tuskless—and hence dangerously malevolent—bull elephant, exiled from the herd and surly, and Father suggested that he and I should, without the others, have the glory of bringing it down.

As we cautiously approached the monster, it picked up our scent and turned to us, raising its trunk formidably and flapping its great ears. Even Father seemed to have a second thought.

"Ambrose, quick! Run back to the others; I can handle this."

And I would have done so! I would! But I was literally paralyzed with panic. My legs were two stone pillars; I couldn't even raise my rifle. The bull was charging now, a thundering black cloud of terror, and I knew my end had come.

I heard the crack of Father's gun, and the huge beast went down, a rolling mass of agony, then suddenly still.

"By God, you're a cool one!" Father cried. "You stood there without blinking. And you were a gentleman, too. You let me have the first go at him when there mightn't have been a second!"

"Oh, I knew you'd bring him down," I heard myself say.

That night I was struck with a fever, which nobody attributed to my trauma, and I was sent back to the base camp. By the time I had recuperated, the safari was over.

❧

The next decade brought great changes and something like peace to my life. In the first place, Father lost the greater part of his by then diminished fortune when the Knickerbocker Trust Company closed its doors in the panic of 1907. There was no longer the possibility of my leading the economically carefree life that he and his brothers had enjoyed; it was now incumbent upon me to earn my own living, which fortunately I was not only happy but relieved to do. After Harvard College, I attended Harvard Law and then secured a good position as a clerk in a leading Wall Street firm.

Father was constantly apologetic that his poor management had condemned me to what he downrated as the passive life of a desk grub. But to me it was the pleasant calm of a dull gray restful heaven after the flickering red of adventure. I believed that my fears and anticipations were over, that I *had* been tested, after all, and not found wanting as a man, and that I could now look forward, like millions of other males, to the routine of a mild usefulness. To cap it all, I married a girl who had the same ambition—or lack of it, as the Vollards undoubtedly would have put it.

Ellen, the child of Long Island neighbors whom I had known and liked since childhood, had always been a quiet little girl, sober and serious, who from her earliest days had known exactly what she wanted from life: a faithful loving husband with a steady job and a nursery full of children. Both of us tended to look at passion and excitement as picturesque storms to be viewed from behind securely closed windows. Ellen got on well with my parents, though I suspect she regarded Father as a little cracked. However, she never said so, and he became very fond of her and doted on the three little children who were born to us in the first five years of our marriage.

The opening of the Great War in 1914 sounded as the knell to bring me back from a decade of illusion to the grim standards of virility. Of course, in the three years of our national neutrality, I was always aware of the chorus of voices in favor of our nonparticipation in the conflict and prayed that they would prevail, but I never doubted that we would ultimately be drawn in. I knew again what I had earlier known: that it was part of my doom.

Needless to say, Father, like his god the Colonel, was howling for war, and he took for granted that I was on his side, nor did I seek for a moment to disillusion him. I accepted my fate with the passivity of despair and could only shrug when Ellen pointed out that if we did go to war, I would surely be exempted as a married man with a family to support.

"Father has received an inheritance from Uncle Tom," I reminded her. "He has already undertaken to support you and the children if I should sign up."

"And leave me with three infants and one of them an asthmatic! If you do that, my love, you'll find the Germans easier to face than the spouse you return to!"

I was beginning to learn that Father was not the only force in my life. And as the carnage in Europe became more and more appalling, with each side sacrificing untold thousands of young men to capture or recapture a few yards of barbed wire,

I started to wonder whether I might not one day rather face Father's wrath than expose myself to it. At night, while Ellen snored mildly at my side, I lay awake, feverishly picturing the mud, the rats, the horrible dawn attacks after an overhead deafening barrage, the stooping rush over barbed wire to bayonet some poor German lad in the guts, or, more likely, to be bayoneted by him, the endless terror and the damp dark waiting, waiting, waiting. And when I slept at last my nightmares were worse. It was almost a relief when we heard the asthmatic gasping of our youngest and had to rise and rush to alleviate his pain.

As soon as Congress had declared war on the central powers, Colonel Roosevelt applied to President Wilson for permission to form his own regiment, in which Father naturally clamored to be included. Of course, the wild offer was turned down, but Father informed me that the Colonel was writing to General Pershing to take his sons Ted and Archie in the first shipments to France and that it might be possible to include me. I had, despite Ellen's first objections, had some military training with Father at the camp at Plattsburg (I had put it to her on the grounds of simple preparedness for any eventuality), and I was now, in a grim mood of acceptance of my destiny, ready to give in to the paternal expectations.

But I faced a kitten who had turned into a tigress.

"Your father and his Colonel make me sick! I wish the President had sent both their superannuated carcasses to France to rot, instead of all the young men on whom our future depends! I'm telling you, Ambrose Vollard, that you are going to apply for exemption from the draft on the perfectly sound and valid ground that you have a large family and a sick baby to support. And that exemption will be granted without question. And not a single solitary soul, except for a couple of crazy Vollards, will either criticize you or think one jot the less of you!"

And that was it. I did what she told me to do. I had become a virtual automaton. My will was crushed.

If that was the ultimate act of cowardice, perhaps the ultimate act of courage lay in my telling Father to his face what I had done.

He said nothing, but his features turned to stone.

Mother intervened. "I think Ambrose is the only person who can be the judge of what he has done, my dear. His decision cannot have been an easy one."

Father closed his eyes and bowed his head. There was another long silence. Finally he made the only comment on the matter he would make to me, then or thereafter.

"I don't know how I am to face the Colonel."

The year that followed, the last of the war, as it turned out, was for me quiet and dull. I was busy at an office badly depleted by men called to the service, and Ellen was, as usual, much occupied with the children, particularly with our asthmatic son, who fortunately was much improved. I was in no way criticized by friends for not being in uniform—there were too many in the same boat—but Ellen and I nonetheless rarely went out at night, content to spend our evenings reading or listening to the radio. Yet my underlying mood was one of consistent if mild depression.

Father treated me, when, as before, Ellen and I dined with him and Mother on Sunday nights, with the same gruff politeness he would have exhibited to any guest at his table. He inquired sympathetically about his grandchildren, sought my opinion politely about the wine he offered, inquired perfunctorily about my law practice, but it was noticeable that he never discussed the war with me. I had wanted no part in it; very well, I would hear nothing of it from him. In a way I was no longer his son. When word came of Quentin Roosevelt's death, his plane shot down behind German lines, he mourned as if Quentin had been his son.

And, of course, I hated it. I may not have been given the white feather by the world, but I knew I deserved it in Father's eyes, and was it not in Father's eyes that I had my real existence? Could I never be free of my obsession? For what reason, now that I had become, inside his mind as well as outside it, the poor creature he had long denied I was, could I not be at liberty to go my own benighted way in peace?

Perhaps I would have, had he not died, shortly after the death of his beloved hero, the great Theodore, in 1919. Both men were worn and prematurely old at only sixty-one. The shock to me was such as to throw me into a kind of nervous breakdown, which might have necessitated my going for a time to a sanatorium, had not a stern talk with my mother formed the beginning of what looked to be a cure, or at least an alleviation.

As I have said, Mother had left my training largely to Father, but I had always known that she still kept an eye on me. Although she never openly challenged her husband's standards, she seemed to live, resolutely if quietly, distinctly apart from them. Of course, the difference in gender explained some of this but not all. She represented to me, when I seemed to be swimming beyond my power of return, the fine, level, sandy beach to which I would be welcome if I could only get back to it.

One evening, calling on her alone, I felt impelled to confide in her all my misery. When I had finished and she gave me a long close look, I realized that I had broken a barrier.

"I have been waiting for you to tell me all this, my child. I haven't ventured to talk basic truths with you until I was sure you were ready to listen. I have always known that you found your father's principles hard to live up to, but I hesitated to interfere, because you acted so determined to work out your problem your own way, and how was I to know that it wasn't the right way? For a man, anyhow. And besides, you seemed to be succeeding, and your father was always so proud of you, and you appeared so devoted to him. Was it a woman's role to barge in and break this up? Mightn't you both have resented it? And rightly, too? But now you present me with a different case. Your father preached one kind of courage. Maybe I can preach another."

"Courage? Oh, not more of that, please, Mother!"

"Just listen, my dear. We can't get around courage. It's at the root of what's wrong with you. Shall I go ahead?"

"Go ahead."

"I warn you. This is going to hurt."

"I'm ready. Shoot."

"You avoided the draft for a perfectly valid reason. You were over thirty, with a family to support and a sick child. Very good. Nobody had a word to say against you, except, of course, your father. That's the given, the *donnée*, as the French critics say."

"And that is correct."

"Except for one thing. Your family wasn't your real reason. Your real reason was that you were afraid to go to war."

I felt like a piece of ice under a steaming hot faucet. Soon there would be nothing left of me. It was all over. At last.

Mother waited for me to speak, but I didn't, so she went on.

"And now comes the real lesson in courage. You must face the fact that you are a man who was afraid to go to war. It's as simple as that. It doesn't mean that you're afraid of everything. You have been brave enough in other things. It means that you were afraid to be killed or mutilated in the most hideous carnage the world has ever seen. You shared that fear with countless others. Some overcame it; some didn't. The world is made up of heroes and non-heroes. They are equally real. Go back, my son, to your real life and your real family, and *live!*"

I felt so immediately lifted up by this clear solution to the problem of a lifetime that I became greedy. How is it that, with salvation in sight, we double our demands for entry?

"Of course, it was easier for Father, wasn't it?"

"What was easier?"

"Why, being brave. He was born brave, wasn't he? He never knew fear. And if you don't know what fear is, is it really so brave to face dragons? Mightn't one be like Siegfried and even like it?"

Mother became very grave at this. "Oh, my Ambrose, lay not that flattering unction to your soul! No one is born fearless. Your father made himself a hero by grit and will power. And don't you ever dare to take it from him!"

I bowed my head in bitter but accepting silence. It was not only myself that I should have to accept; it was she as well. The man she really admired, the man she would always admire, was Father. That was what I would have to live with: that I could never compete in a woman's eyes with a hero. Was I even sure that Ellen, deep down, didn't share that feeling? No, I was not sure.

The Heiress

WHEN WALTER DIED, shortly after the atomic bomb that ended World War II, in the terrible course of which his exhausting diplomatic missions to allied and neutral nations had fatally weakened his old heart, several publishers tried to interest me in writing a widow's account of our life in public affairs. But Walter had already published a Pulitzer Prize–winning memoir of his career as a foreign affairs expert and roving ambassador, in the foreword to which he had, with his usual graciousness, acknowledged his "never-to-be-forgotten debt to a wife and partner whose value to me in my hours of toil and rest can never be adequately expressed." That is about all a consort of my era—and though I was a decade younger than Walter, I was born in 1880—can expect as a tribute to marital services that, like those of the bulk of my contemporaries, amounted to little more than a footnote to their husbands' careers. That is not to say that Walter Wheelock was not a perfect gentleman, a faithful and devoted spouse, one who encouraged me in all my interests and hobbies. It was just the way things were. I was always aware—and I am sure he was, though it was never mentioned—that the only real boost he got from me in his rise to the top was the money for which he had married me.

If I had had children, I wouldn't have written that. Why

should I wish to hurt their feelings? But this memoir, which, if read at all, will be read posthumously in some historical archive, will have no value to anyone unless it is strictly true. So I may as well put it on the line, that it was widely accepted in my day, both here and abroad, that any ambitious and impecunious young man who elected to enter an unremunerative career, such as government, teaching, the armed forces or even the church, would do well to avail himself of a dowry. In Europe this was frankly spoken of as an accepted thing, but in New York, where persistent lip service was given—uptown, if not downtown—to romantic notions, it was distinctly muted. This was the cause of considerable confusion and much unhappiness to some of our young heiresses who wanted to be loved for themselves. In Europe they wanted only to be loved—it didn't so much matter for what. All I can say for myself is that I was a bit more of a realist than my sisters and cousins. At least I got a good man. Perhaps a great one.

Who or what I was or thought I was, as a young girl, appears to be what today is called an identity crisis. I was and still am rarely mentioned in any social column without the added legend "a grandchild of Samuel Thorn." That was and is, of course, also true of my siblings and of my first cousins on Mother's side of the family, that cheerful, boisterous group of youngsters who in our youth stuck so harmoniously together in our neighborhood of brownstone mansions up and down Fifth Avenue. They were the offspring of Mother and her sisters: Sewards (that's us), Hammerslys and Degeners, and of her brother, Samuel Thorn, Jr., almost a society of their own, united in friendly and loving awe of Grandpa and Grandma Thorn, smug and smiling in their immense chocolate-colored cube of a residence. You can see the latter today in my living room, in the conversation piece by Seymour Guy, facing each other complacently in opposite armchairs, hands in lap, surrounded by walls cluttered with academic canvases. Grandpa was known to the public as simply the richest man in the world.

Yet it was still important that I was *not* a Thorn; I was a Seward. Mother, of course, had been a Thorn, and we lived in a house adjoining Grandpa's, waited on by a staff of fifteen, but I never regarded my branch as wealthy. Children look up the social ladder, rarely down, and we all knew, and fully accepted, that Grandpa was intent on establishing a dynasty in his name and that Uncle Sam had already received half his fortune and could look forward one day to receiving the rest, minus the settlements on his sisters, which, however small in relation to his own, would have been considered princely in any land of accepted primogeniture. We children learned exactitude in using the vocabulary of wealth. I never, for example, considered myself an "heiress." That in our world denoted a dowry of ten million and up. Mother was an heiress, yes, but she had four children to divide an inheritance much diminished by Papa's lavish spending. In my generation Uncle Sam's daughters, Beatrice and Diana, were the real heiresses and could marry European dukes if they chose — or were chosen—while we other granddaughters would have to make do with humbler mates.

Not that I minded these distinctions. I have always been devoted to Beatrice, who found happiness in a second marriage, and to Diana, who survives to this day in a renowned and rather bristling virginity. But the situation was somewhat complicated by the fact that *I* was the one who was supposed to be

Grandpa's favorite. Yet I never ascribed this to personal merit, nor did I expect any compensation for the status. It was a role that had been handed me by a quixotic deity in the skies who might just as well have given it to any other grandchild. There was no cause for pride on my part or jealousy on anyone else's. When I was told to run next door to Grandpa's, where the smiling butler behind the bronze grille awaited me, because Grandpa wanted to show me off to his breakfast business guests, I would scurry into the dining room and raise my round little face to be kissed by a rotund, balding, thickly whiskered old gentleman with glinting piggy eyes and a smell of tobacco, and be called his "darling Aggie-Baggie." I recognized it as a kind of charade of homely piety, and that once I was dismissed with a friendly little pat on my rump, the great man would totally forget me in the resumption of his business discussions.

That different adult males should play different roles in the family drama did not strike me as inconsistent. It was the way things were. Papa, for example, saw Grandpa, his father-in-law, through lenses not adjusted to the more general family view. He used to say—and he was never one to lower his voice or spare anyone's feelings—that the "Thorn tribe" of my siblings and cousins tended to cling together because the reputation of Grandpa Thorn's deceased father, to whom Papa referred unceremoniously as "that old pirate," was still sufficiently odorous to keep the Knickerbocker families at bay, and that even the cloak of Seward respectability (we were dimly related to Lincoln's Secretary of State) that Papa had provided for his own offspring would not wholly shield us from the snubs of Livingstons and Van Rensselaers. But looking back on that era, I can see that only the stuffiest of the old guard would hold themselves aloof from a crowd of good-looking and amiable youngsters who had money to spend and large country estates for congenial house parties. Even people who shunned Grandma's receptions were happy to have their issue play with and ultimately marry her grandchildren.

But Papa never changed his mind, never altered a position once taken. I see him now in the solid marble bust so out of scale with the rest of my apartment. How the round eyeballs over the strong aggressive nose and flared nostrils seem to glare! From the richly thick wavy hair and tall formidable brow down to the pointed moustache and trim goatee and to the astrachan collar of his frock coat, it is only too clear that you are faced with the type of American orator or statesman of his day, as seen in those dreadful statues in the rotunda of the Capitol in Washington. Except that Papa was not a statesman; he only dreamed of being one. He had been president of a street car company that went bankrupt because he would not allow the cars to operate on the sabbath, and he had managed, by the extravagance of his residences in town and country, to go through all of Mother's money that was not nailed down in trust. But he had fought gallantly as a cavalry colonel in the Civil War, and as a leader of civic groups he had thundered impressively and ineffectually against the corruption of the age. It never occurred to any of his three daughters that he could be disobeyed or criticized. It did occur, however, to his only son.

My brother, Otto, had none of Papa's vigor or much of the *joie de vivre* of our cousins. He was tall and skinny and highly critical of almost everything. I'm afraid that he hated Papa, and that his feeling was richly returned.

"He thinks he's such a god among men," Otto would observe sourly to me. "But he's really only a figurehead on the pedestal of Grandpa's money."

I, as the eldest daughter, was chosen to take the place of honor in Papa's life that Otto declined. This only confirmed the childhood impression, already created by Grandpa's favoritism, that my life was a series of sets before which I, like a professional monologist, was to enact certain prescribed roles. As the great Ruth Draper, whom I was later so to admire, would in one scene be an empty-headed debutante and in another the wife of a miner lost in a cave-in, so I had the different but equally factitious parts to play of the idolized grandchild and the adoring daughter. It wasn't that I found the parts difficult to perform, but I was afflicted at times with the haunting sense that there was no Agnes Seward left of me when I had to run off stage into the wings.

One could argue, of course, that I was no different from Grandpa or Papa, who were also playing roles. Certainly Papa enjoyed responding to the image of the virgin priestess daughter who would love him more than she would any swain, who might indeed elect to remain permanently unwed to tend the paternal shrine, an Iphigenia, who in the Racine tragedy that I always detested, assents docilely to her father's demand that she be sacrificed to bring winds to the becalmed Grecian fleet. But it was always evident to me that neither Grandpa nor Papa suffered from any loss of identity when the curtain dropped. They were only too visibly strong and definite characters in the "real world," which the former dominated and the latter tried to.

Sometimes I would speculate that it was a matter of gender; that men were not acting, that off stage as well as on they were the same persons, that it was my own poor sex who had to learn our parts in the play that duplicated the lives of our masters. Yet even here there was an "out" for some fortunate ladies. I use the term "ladies" advisedly, for this "out" was evidently not available to humbler females. Mother and her sisters were "heiresses" and did not have to perform before the footlights; they could remain, serene and placid, in their big brownstones or Beaux Arts country châteaux, or migrate on set dates to distant villas appropriate to the changing season, and live for clothes and cards in overheated conservatories filled with palms and marble fauns. The sputterings of their sometimes irascible husbands dashed like spray against the rocks of their tranquillity; they were too confident that nothing the latter could do would undermine the eternity of solid support guaranteed by their father's limitless fortune.

It was in the year after my debut, a time when it was generally expected that a young lady of decent looks and ample fortune should take a mate, that I learned of a third role that I was perhaps destined to play. It was Papa who revealed this to me. He did not, after all, it appeared, wish me to remain a virgin priestess at his altar. Far from it! He wished me to marry, not one of what he called "the silly fops you and your cousins play around with" or even one of the golden heirs of our circle; oh, no, he wanted me to marry a "great man," or one who bore the signs of becoming—a statesman, an ambassador, a many-starred general!

He confided in me gravely that I was the only one among his offspring who had any of his brains and talent. He described my two poor younger sisters as giddy and party-obsessed, and I have already written what he thought of Otto. He predicted that, as the partner of greatness, I could make a contribution to history and that it was a woman's only way. But wasn't he in fact preparing the sole poor candidate he had to attain the success that had consistently eluded him? Did he love me? Could he? And did I love him? Really and truly? Certainly he frightened me, but he also awed me. I had always been flattered by his attention, which made me feel pleasantly superior to my siblings. Now I began to wonder whether I was getting too much of it.

He and I had in common a love of reading; his happiest, or perhaps I should say his least frustrated, hours were spent in his dark leathery library, whose walls were covered from floor to ceiling with shelves of closely packed volumes, including the rare quartos and folios of his favorite Jacobean dramatists. He liked to read aloud to me from the latter, and, though impressed by his noble tone and theatrical emphasis, I was sometimes appalled at the blood and thunder he admired. I can still hear him in Malcolm's speech in *Macbeth*.

> Nay, had I power, I should
> Pour the sweet milk of concord into hell,
> Uproar the universal peace, confound
> All unity on earth.

Was that what Papa would do if *he* were a great man? Was there a wish under all his oratory to wreak revenge on the universe? At any rate, after his first pronouncement of the desirability of my ultimate union with a gentleman of national importance, he did not mention the subject again, and I am fairly sure that he never discussed it with Mother or any of her family. I began to wonder, with some relief, whether it had been a momentary fancy on his part. I should have known better.

It was my cousin Lily Hammersly, Aunt Maud's daughter and my exact contemporary (we had "come out" together in a joint ball given by Grandpa and Grandma), who came closest to convincing me that life didn't have to be as I or even as Papa visualized it. She was considered the "belle" of the family, though her little brown pert face was not much prettier than my rather pallid blondness. But she had animation and high spirits and wit, and wasn't in the least in awe of anyone, even Grandpa, whom she dared to tease, or Papa, her uncle-in-law, who was strangely tolerant of her even when she contradicted one of his pronouncements. She regarded the older generations as obstacles that could be made to yield to cajolery, and all of the cousinage depended on her to extract permission for whatever outing or other project that, without her, might be subject to family veto.

In the first year after our coming-out, Lily's interest vested exclusively in the young men who called at our houses on afternoons when our parents received and among whom it was expected we should ultimately find a spouse. Needless to say, Lily's temperament led her to entertain highly romantic ideals, and she had little patience with the concept of an "arranged match." She also had little patience with my mild preference for Winthrop, or "Wintie," Tillinghast, who was the most assiduous of my not madly assiduous beaux.

"He's too old and too stuffy, Aggie," she insisted. "He's like Osric in *Hamlet.* He genuflected to his mother's dug before he sucked it."

Lily was not only well read; she was very free with her literary allusions. But she had a point. Wintie was certainly older;

he was thirty plus to my nineteen and already established as a junior officer in the bank that handled the Thorn trusts. He was tall and perhaps too dignified, with a regular, rather immobile countenance and prematurely gray hair, but he had a surprising sense of humor and a kindly manner. He knew everybody, was well liked and a popular leader of cotillions. The Tillinghasts were not rich but were well connected, and his two elder brothers had married substantial fortunes. I classified him as the kind of man who, even if he had to marry money, would marry only a rich girl he sincerely loved. That was a distinction that most of my female cousins learned to make early. I was very fond of Wintie and tended to resent Lily's aspersions, but she did alter my vision of him.

We used sometimes to take afternoon callers next door to see Grandpa's great picture gallery, and once, when Wintie and I found ourselves alone there, we had a colloquy that irritated me.

Of course, the paintings that Grandpa so lovingly collected are all—or almost all; some of his canvases by Corot and Millais are still admired—subject to public ridicule today. They tended to be academic and what was then considered realistic: Meissonier's Napoleonic battles gleaming with brandished swords and rustling with charging horse; elegant Roman dames by Alma-Tadema gazing down at blue seas from marble balustrades; stout cardinals drinking champagne in paneled parlors by Vibert. I quite accepted the high estimate of the gallery by family and friends and took it for granted that although Leonardo and Michelangelo may have produced greater art, it was because it was locked away in museums that it had not been lured across the Atlantic by Grandpa's checkbook.

Wintie took his stand for several minutes before a picture by Gérôme entitled *Thumbs Down*, depicting a scene in the Roman arena where a victorious gladiator, astride the stricken body of his antagonist, appeals to the audience for that which will bid him to dispatch or spare his victim. The Vestal Virgins, seated in a unit by the railing, are unanimous for death, while in the imperial box above them, Marcus Aurelius, conspicuously indifferent to the outcome, is seen giving his total attention to the perusal of some learned scroll.

"It's a wonderful painting!" Wintie exclaimed. "You can see so clearly the attitude of the imperial philosopher. He will never neglect his official duties, one of which is to lend his presence to the popular diversions of his people. On the other hand he is disgusted by the bloody spectacle and sees no reason to lose time from the learned studies that enhance his administrative talents."

"But why can't he at least save that poor man's life?" I demanded.

"Because he believes he shouldn't interfere. *Panem et circenses*—that's what kept the people happy. Without them, there was no telling what civil unrest might occur. The man who had the whole civilized world to govern couldn't be concerned with the life of one gladiator."

"Civilized! I'm glad you call it that! A great man would have taken one position or another. He would have joined in the applause and the decisions, or he would have stopped the games altogether. Napoleon would have. Lincoln would have."

"President Lincoln was something of a compromiser, Miss Seward. And always a realist."

"Do you think he would have put up with this? Never! And anyway I can't see a man, a real man, sitting in his box reading Plato or Zeno while dwarfs armed with spears and nets battled barbarian women with sabers." Perhaps I had been reading too much Lew Wallace or Bulwer-Lytton. And then it occurred to me that I could imagine Papa taking an interest in such conflicts; in Madrid, he had adored the bullfights. And I could even see Grandpa putting a stop to the whole business. But to do nothing! "Only a woman would act like Marcus Aurelius!" I went on to protest, not caring whether Wintie took this personally.

But he only chuckled. "My dear Miss Seward, may I point out that it is the Vestals who are condemning the poor man who has lost his round?"

"Maybe that's what happens to us poor women when the men won't take any position!"

But there was another picture in the gallery, also depicting a scene in the Colosseum, that was my particular favorite. The legend on its frame was *The Last Token*, and it showed a young woman, barefoot and clad in a plain white gown, standing alone on the sandy floor of the arena, with nothing between her and the two snarling felines emerging from the lifted grilled gate. But she pays no heed to the hungry beasts; her eyes are searching the front row boxes for the noble lover who has just tossed her a farewell rose. It was not long after this colloquy with Wintie that I found myself again alone in Grandpa's gallery with a young man who was skillfully attempting to replace Wintie in my still rather smothered affections. He was Miles Constable, the possessor of a florid manner and many smiles who tended to make fun of everything and almost everybody. I thought he overdid this, but he intrigued me.

He knew of my preference among the paintings and was re-examining *The Last Token* with a critical eye.

"Do you really admire this daub, Aggie?" He had dropped the address "Miss Seward" as early as our second meeting. "What a cad the poor girl's lover must have been! I presume he was a noble and she a Christian, and that it was his loose tongue that betrayed her secret to the police. Unless he was tired of their liaison and tipped them off about her Sunday visits to the catacombs to hear Mass."

"That's so like you, Miles! Always to attribute the lowest motive to anyone! Her lover hadn't been condemned, because he wasn't a Christian. What could he do against the might of Rome but stay as near to her as he could until the end and show her that he would never forget her? It would take more courage than I have to see my loved one torn to pieces. That rose he tossed to her was like the crucifix that a holy monk braved the flames to hold up to the eyes of the dying Joan of Arc!"

"Only your Marcus Pomposus, or whatever his name was, wasn't risking his well-pressed toga in any fire. He was probably too busy passing sweetmeats to his new girlfriend in the imperial box."

"What could you expect him to do? Jump into the arena and feed himself to those leopards?"

"They're not leopards; they're jaguars. I noted that the first time you introduced me to this chamber of horrors. You may ask what jaguars were doing in the Colosseum centuries before the discovery of South America. Well, I made a point of reading up on the Viennese painter who executed your masterpiece and discovered that he used animals in the local zoo for his models, obviously without checking on their usual habitat."

"Very clever of you." It was like Miles to know everything. "But I wonder whether you're not like that Roman lord yourself. I can see you, sitting calmly in that box—oh, possibly with a stray tear quickly brushed away—and flicking with your fingers one perfect rose at the unfortunate but soon-to-be-forgotten girl. After all, wasn't it folly on her part to get mixed up with those preachy, lower-class Christians? And to think I criticized Wintie Tillinghast for admiring Marcus Aurelius in the Gérôme picture! At least the emperor turned his eyes from bloodshed to a learned tract!"

"Except Wintie Tillingsnob would be turning his eyes to Colonel Mann's Society Notes. Whereas I would have leaped over the railing of my box in a futile attempt to lure away the jaguars with those same sweetmeats you saw me offering to the high-born Roman damsel sitting by me. And when the disgusted jaguars had eaten me instead, an amused Caligula or Nero would have freed you from the arena and invited you to an imperial orgy."

"*Me?* Why me? Am I the girl in the arena?"

"Aren't you? Isn't that why you're drawn to the ghastly picture?"

I blushed. He was uncanny. It was what made people uneasy about him. "We all have our fantasies, I suppose," I muttered. "Harmless fantasies."

"Are they so harmless? Mightn't they be keys to our personality? Might it not be significant that Agnes Seward sees herself as a martyr?"

"You really think me such an idiot?"

"I don't see you as an idiot at all." Miles was suddenly serious, a rare pose for him. If it *was* a pose. "I see you as a very perceptive person in an unperceptive world. And if you ever should be a martyr, you'd be a brave one."

I found the odd compliment almost exhilarating. Yet there was apprehension in my reaction as well. Why should Miles have the gift of probing so deeply behind the masks we all had to wear? If it was my fate to play different roles in a tragedy or comedy with whose composition and direction I had had nothing to do, was it not somehow in the cards that the production should end in a martyrdom? If the last act was not to end in a guffaw, should it not terminate on a scaffold? Wasn't anything else banal, presumptuous, even irreligious? And didn't a tragedy have to begin with a seeming success?

Miles Constable looked younger than his thirty years. He was short and verging on plump, with a clear, fresh, boyish countenance, a smile constantly on his red, full lips, thick wavy chestnut hair and an effervescence of spirit. Had he been taller and more slender, he might have suggested a romantic poet, a Shelley; as it was, one was more put in mind of a cherub, who, like the mythical Dionysus, was capable of impish, perhaps even sinister tricks. Miles had no visible employment nor any known private income to explain his expensive tweeds, his ruby cufflinks, the elegant little dinner parties that he hosted in Delmonico's, and it was rumored that he was not above taking commissions from the grocers and decorators and wine merchants whose products he recommended to his rich friends. And furthermore, there was no recognized family of respectable Constables he could claim as his own. Yet he was never spoken of with the mild contempt that society reserves for its most coddled sycophants. Miles was taken seriously by the great dames of Manhattan society and was not scorned by even the most Philistine of their husbands. They sought him in every capacity but that of son-in-law.

Now what explained this? I think they may have feared his wit and his startling insight into the most carefully hidden traits of character. My comparison to Dionysus was not casual. There was a legend that this god had survived the pagan era and had inhabited medieval Catholic Europe in disguise. People who met him felt his charm and the amiable freedom of his manners and ways, but they also felt the chill, as from another era, of a system of opposite values that vaguely but ominously threatened them. Maybe it was that Miles, in the traditional role of social climber, never seemed to climb, and that in the expected guise of a flatterer he rarely paid compliments. If Miles really wanted something, what did he really want?

In his dealings with any pretty young woman he played—amusingly, never offensively, even rather delightfully—the role of a swain smitten by her charms. I enjoyed the game when he played it with me, and I was startled and excited—though I didn't believe it—when my cousin Lily Hammersly confided in me that she thought Miles was less joking and more in earnest with me than with others.

"But why should that be?" I demanded.

"I assume he thinks the time has come to get married. Don't they all?"

"And what makes me the lucky girl?"

"Because he's in love with you, silly."

"Maybe he's in love with what he imagines to be my money."

"Oh, they all want money. That's what the French call the *donnée*. We're not above it ourselves, are we? The Thorns, I mean. How did Descartes put it: *Je dépense; donc je suis?* That's me all over."

"But Lily, *love?* What about that?"

"Do you think money rules out love? Dream on, dear."

Well, such an idea was intensely interesting to any girl of nineteen, and I was no exception. Miles immediately became the principal preoccupation of my agitated mind and spirits, and a strong sentiment for him soon bit the heels of my temporary doubts. Was there a real Miles under the cynical wit, the perennial extra man? And would he be real to me when he was only a jester in the court of the great Mrs. Astor?

I had, as must now be clear, little basic confidence in my own attractions. I may have been blond and blue-eyed and made a pleasant enough impression when I entered a room, but brother Otto used to observe, in his sour fashion, that I had bad bone structure and would probably have a pancake face at thirty and that I'd better catch a man while I could. I became what I considered engagingly coy at Mile's advances.

"You pretend to find me bold and brassy," he told me, as we sat out a dance at Lily's younger sister's coming-out ball, "but you don't. In fact, I rather intrigue you, don't I?"

"And just what, besides your elephantine ego, gives you that idea?"

"Because you intrigue *me*. And girls who do that are apt to find me really intriguing."

"But you've heard of exceptions that prove the rule."

"Agnes Seward, haven't you divined by now that I'm considering proposing to you? And do you think I'd do that if I had any reason to believe you didn't have the sense to find me charming?"

"Propose to me! Are you in a position to propose to anyone? Can you support a family?"

"No, but you can."

"*Merci du compliment!* Anyway, that would depend on what Papa would do for me. And it's not likely that he would approve of you. Why, you don't even have a job!"

"Well, I wouldn't throw away your money the way he has your mother's."

I should have got up and walked away. But I didn't, and his horrid smile took full advantage of my indecision.

"How dare you speak of my father like that!"

"Everyone knows it. Certainly everyone who knows Otto."

"Otto is outrageous."

"Let's leave that aside. Will you marry me?"

"Of course not."

"Shall we dance?"

"I think we'd better."

And we danced. But from then on our relationship was distinctly changed. He was—to me—a declared suitor and a constant caller at the house. My parents were not aware of his intentions; I can now see that they probably considered him a confirmed bachelor, or even a pederast, though the latter term was unknown to me at the time. Papa did, however, see fit to warn me of Miles's complete ineligibility.

"Mr. Constable is a pleasant enough addition to any dinner party, Agnes. But don't get into your head the idea that he could ever, by the remotest possibility, be considered an appropriate mate for any of your circle. He is jobless and penniless and has no purpose in life but to amuse himself and others. Such men end up either in the gutter or marrying rich women. I don't know which fate is worse."

This was quite in keeping with what I expected of Papa; it was obviously in keeping with his role in my life. But I was beginning to suspect that Miles might be offering me something different and more interesting, no matter that it was fraught with unfamiliarity and danger. I had never had much feeling that the men in control of my world were necessarily right or wrong. They were the powers that were; that was all. But the question—*was* it all?—was never totally banned from my speculations. One answer may have been that I was a pagan: I believed in gods, all right—how could I not, when thunderbolts so often threatened—but it did not follow that the gods were beneficent, or that a less black-browed one might not occasionally surface. I remembered Dionysus.

There was, however, an aspect of Miles that bothered me greatly, and that was the somber side of his nature, which I had not known before and which showed itself more sharply as his courtship (for that was what I now fully recognized it to be) progressed. He seemed to have a dark sense, which made me uneasy, that I, in some strange fashion, represented his "last chance."

"I don't see why you undervalue yourself," I protested to him once. "It seems to me that you make too much of your disadvantages in life. You have all kinds of abilities. Everyone says that! You could go into business."

"There speaks the tycoon's granddaughter! Me, in business? Can you imagine it? I'd go mad after my first week in the counting house. And so would my poor supervisors."

"Well, you could be a lawyer. Or a doctor."

"Agnes, I'm thirty-two! And utterly untrained for law or for medicine. Don't you see it? I'm in a world that has no use for me—commercially, professionally, even artistically. I'm a fifth wheel in Mr. McKinley's America."

"You get on. Look how well you get on!"

"From hand to mouth. Until the first day I bore Old Lady Astor. Or Alva Belmont. Or Mamie Fish. And then my goose is cooked."

"But it's still very tasty, I'm sure."

"Laugh on. I'd be indigestible. Always overdone. No, I'm like you, Aggie. We don't belong."

"What do you mean, *I* don't belong? It seems to me, if anything, I belong too much."

"On the surface, yes. But it's not only you, dear child. It's you and your siblings and the whole tribe of your cousins—all of your grandpa's multitudinous progeny. Let's take them, one by one. We'll start with your brother, Otto, a weakling, a doomed failure ..."

"Otto is brilliant! You've said so yourself!"

"What has that got to do with it? I'm speaking of character. Otto is twenty-five and hasn't done a thing in his life but hate his father. That's an interesting occupation, but hardly a life's work. Your cousins Jack and Billy Hammersly are already on their way to the devil—Jack with drink and Billy with gambling. Oh, they're both charming and still young, and everyone smilingly assumes they'll straighten out, but a sharp eye can see what the end will be. Sammy Thorn is somewhat steadier, for he's being trained to be the rich one, but he wholly lacks the imagination to handle a fortune, and his undiscriminating susceptibility to designing women almost guarantees that he'll marry a gold digger who'll make a dent even in his pile. As for his brother Alistair, he's ..."

"But what about the girls?" I interrupted indignantly. "You can't say any of them drink or gamble."

"No, they're better off, I admit. The stronger sex always

is. But they'll still be married, every one of them, for their money."

"You can't know how that worries them! They'll be cautious about that, never fear!"

"It won't do them a particle of good, because they expect mercenary men to be greasy moustache-twisters and not broad-shouldered, blond, blue-eyed Yankee Adonises. Some of the girls, of course, may marry peers, whose money motives, for reasons of pure snobbery, are forgiven by their fathers, but they will be miserable if not salvaged by divorce or annulment. The lucky ones will marry solid burghers who will be content with their dowries and leave their spouses to enjoy cards and clothes while they engross themselves in a stock market that doubles the money they can never learn to enjoy."

"Oh, you're terrible! And what do you leave for me? What do *you* offer that's so great? Aren't you as much after money as the others? Why, you don't even have the decency to make a secret of it!"

"I don't!" Miles jumped to his feet and spread his arms out as if to embrace the gilded little French salon in which I had chosen to receive him. "But I'd use your money to get you out of all this! To make you free! To make us both free!"

"And you're the only man who can give me this freedom?"

"You know, I really think I am. The only man, anyway, who can give it to you and love you at the same time. It's a rare chance, Aggie. You'd better grab it!"

And I believed him! I still, looking back, believe him. Had I thought myself a free agent, I wonder whether I shouldn't have accepted him then and there. But I had to consult my parents, and that night I went to Mama, who hardly listened to me before sending me straight to Papa's study. And there all hell broke loose.

What I had to make clear to my parents was that Miles was now presenting himself as a suitor for my hand. I had by no means made up my mind as to whether I would ultimately accept or deny his suit, but I did not feel that I could allow my family to continue to receive him under the illusion that he was just another Sunday afternoon caller. I suppose I should not have been surprised that Papa failed utterly to understand my noncommittal attitude. He assumed, with his usual violence, that I was already in passion's grip and that I might be expected to climb down a rope ladder one night from my third-floor bedroom to the pavement on Fifth Avenue to elope with Miles, presumably clutching, like Jessica in *The Merchant of Venice*, as many of the family jewels and ducats as I could get my hot little hands on.

"I have always taken pride in your intelligence and common sense, Agnes," he barked at me. "I have regarded you as a striking exception to the weakness to which your sex is lamentably subject. And you *know* what plans I had for you! But now you have shown yourself one of the very weakest of women! That *man*—if the term applies to him—will not be received under this roof again! And I forbid you to meet him elsewhere."

"What am I to do, then? Not go out at all? For Miles goes to all the parties I go to. And he's Sammy Thorn's best friend. How am I to avoid meeting him?"

Papa appeared temporarily nonplussed by the coolness of

my logic. But he came up with an answer. "I mean you should not see him alone. Or by appointment. If you attend a party, and he comes in and joins the group of which you are a part, I suppose you shouldn't make a scene by refusing to nod to him. But let there be no going into corners for tête-à-têtes!"

"But, Papa, what if the group breaks up, and I'm left alone with him?"

"Don't ask such silly questions!" he exclaimed in exasperation. "I want your intimacy with that scoundrel to cease. How it's to be done I leave to you. What are your brains for, I'd like to know?"

I knew when to stop. I had got all the leeway I needed. I didn't want to push Papa into sending me up the Hudson to stay with his two dismal maiden sisters in their bleak Gothic tower. And I soon learned that the surest way to placate him and to avert his watchful eye from my comings and goings was to treat with common courtesy any new candidate that he brought forward to displace Miles from what he called my "obsession."

And he soon enough had one. In fact, it became apparent that the true cause of Papa's unreasonable and ungoverned fit of temper over poor Miles was less the latter's marital ineligibility than the untimeliness of his proposal, coming as it did at the moment when Papa had at last selected his own candidate for the honor of my hand. The "great man" of the future, his and mine, was to be Walter Wheelock.

The most extraordinary thing about Walter—and he was a most extraordinary man—was that nobody, including me, ever really got to know him, ever fathomed the depths of his arcane personality. The almost impenetrable personality he turned to the world and, with only a few changes, to his immediate circle was a gracious but formal one: that of a tall, slender, handsome man, with a strong chin, a commanding nose, piercing eyes and a high clear forehead reaching up to a balding yet noble scalp. But if he was gracious to the world, it was also apparent that he expected to conquer it.

Papa had told me his history. The offspring of two old but impecunious Manhattan families, he had been raised by a widowed mother who had denied herself every luxury in order to give him the best of schooling, clothes and travel. And he had rewarded her every expectation: leading his class at Yale, being "tapped" for the prestigious secret society, Skull & Bones, writing a best seller on the history of the Monroe Doctrine at twenty-five, and having now earned, still in his early thirties, the reputation of being one of the brightest and most coming young men in the State Department. Papa admitted to only a single check in Walter's rising career: that of being rejected as a suitor for the hand of my cousin Beatrice Thorn, the great heiress of the family, by her father on the grounds that he was a fortune hunter. Papa's low opinion of Uncle Sam Thorn had dropped even lower when he learned of this.

"Your brother is an even greater ass than I suspected," he fumed to my placid and indifferent mother at the breakfast table. "He cannot see the difference between a man who seeks a solid financial basis for a career that may lead to his being Secretary of State and one who is looking for money to keep himself in racehorses and mistresses."

Yet Walter must have been enough of a realist to revise downward the estimate of his financial requirements, for he evidently saw no objection to my less brilliant expectations. And I can certainly assert that from the very beginning of his attentions to me, when he assumed the infelicitous role of suitor into which my father, with his customary absence of any concession to subtlety, had thrust him, he tactfully refrained from all adulatory compliments or factitiously romantic phrases. He could, by his easy, cool manners, have been an old family friend or a relative, a pleasant bridge between the generations (he was halfway between Mama's age and mine) and a gentleman who did not consider a lady his conversational inferior. I can see in retrospect that there may have been a shrewd design in his letting me see him as the precise opposite of Miles (whose name he never mentioned), as a man, in short, who sought to reorganize the world rather than sneer at it, and as a guide to fit a woman into the new creation rather than fly with her out of it to some never-never land. And he did succeed in weakening my prejudice against him as a paternal candidate; I came to accept him, not certainly as a lover, but as a new friend.

Walter's views on the role of women in our society were considerably more liberal than those of my father and uncles. While he did not rule out a future for us in the professions or in business, he believed that at present our best hope was to be the wives and helpmates of important men.

"There's no point in getting too far ahead of the times," he told me. "If I were a woman, I'd want to marry a man whose career I could share. It wouldn't be a businessman. What role is there for a Mrs. Rockefeller or a Mrs. Carnegie to play, in oil or in steel? But in politics and diplomacy, the husband and wife can be almost equal partners. That is something some of our First Ambassadresses have learned better than some of our First Ladies."

This faintly irritated me. It was too much of his plan to

show me all I could do for *him*, and it gave me the nerve to twit him with the rumored engagement of his former inamorata.

"Well, at least we know one kind of marriage that is a true partnership," I affirmed. "My cousin Beatrice and the Earl of Chester. Aren't lords and ladies equal stars in the ceremony of an ancient peerage?"

"They could be. Perhaps they *should* be. But American brides don't always do their part; they don't believe in it."

"Beatrice will. She loves coronets and tiaras!"

"As bangles, yes. But wait till she sees great gobs of her fortune going to pay the earl's pile of old debts and to set up his younger brothers. And wait till he wants to use the money she's designed for a splendid new mansion in London on some moldy old castle in a remote part of Wales."

I must admit that things turned out for Beatrice much as he predicted. She ultimately found happiness in a second union, with her oldest son's tutor.

Miles, of course, was forbidden our house, as well as the homes of Mama's sisters, but Uncle Sam Thorn would listen neither to hints nor bold requests from his siblings: Miles Constable was a friend of his son Sammy, and no friend of Sammy's was to be denied access to the big reproduction of Blois in which Grandpa's principal heir resided. Lily Hammersly would alert me to when Miles was going there, and he and I had many a forbidden tête-à-tête under the palms of the dank conservatory.

Miles was taking his banishment from the distaff Thorn establishments more bitterly than I had expected; he obviously resented what he called my passivity under the paternal interdict, and he was most sarcastic about Walter.

"Though I have to admit that your old man has chosen cleverly," he conceded. "Even rather devilishly. Wheelock doesn't fit into any of the categories of fortune hunters about which I warned you. Not, of course, that he isn't a fortune hunter. But he does offer something besides his greed."

"I suppose that's big of you. What is it that he offers?"

"Well, I imagine he'd be a faithful spouse. He's too cold for anything else. And I don't think he'd waste your money. He's too careful for that. He might even be a good father. There's only one thing he'd never be able to give you."

He paused, until I asked him: "What?"

"Oh, a little thing that some people think makes the world go 'round."

But it irritated me that he should so blandly take for granted not only that love was what I needed but that Walter was any less capable of providing it than he was.

"So there *is* one little thing that the ever scornful Miles Constable doesn't scorn!"

"There is," he replied, with uncharacteristic complacency. "And that little thing is love. Wheelock can't give it because he hasn't got it to give. He's like Alberich in *The Ring*. He's given up love in exchange for power."

"And how do you know that I don't agree with him that it's a good bargain?" I was exasperated with Miles, perhaps with his whole sex. "How do you know that I'm not a Thorn through and through? How do you know that the only thing that will make me happy isn't to be in a position like Grandpa's, where he can say to one man 'go' and he goeth and to another 'come' and he cometh?"

"Oh, Aggie, don't joke about this. You'd be a lost thing

without love! Why don't we run off together and get married and live in Florence for a year? I could just afford it, and then your family would be bound to come around. They always do, after the first baby!"

And do you know, if he hadn't laughed that high screeching laugh of his, I might have done it? For laugh or no laugh, he still loved me. I was always, oddly enough, sure of that. And my feeling for him was always bubbling up, never quite high enough, because of my constant sense that he wasn't quite real, wasn't a man a Seward or a Thorn *could* marry, but there might not have needed too great a change of circumstances to push me over the dam. Anyway, that laugh annoyed me sufficiently to make me rise and go home.

There, I was confronted with an irate father who had discovered my trysts with Miles and decreed that I should leave at once for a Caribbean cruise on our yacht, *The Osprey*, with Mama and my sisters. He would join us later in Nassau. On the deep blue sea amid the emerald isles I would have the opportunity to contemplate all the possible consequences of my persisting in such rash and disobedient conduct.

I was in a desperately sullen mood during the cruise and would hardly exchange more than monosyllables with my family at meals. There were days when I declined to go ashore and would sit on the fantail with an unopened book in my lap. My reluctance to leave the ship, however, received Mama's support when she discovered that we were being followed by Sammy Thorn, Jr., in his beautiful sailing yacht, and that he had Miles Constable on board!

This chase, if chase it was, was picked up by a society reporter, who wrote a lurid tale about it in a New York evening paper, which brought down upon us a series of irate cables from my furious sire at home. The reporter had great sport with his account of the two great pleasure crafts plying the waves of the Caribbean, carrying the pursuer Theseus and the pursued Ariadne. Mama at last expressed herself with a tight-lipped severity almost unknown to her usually bland and accommodating nature.

"I'd rather see you in your grave than married to that man."

And then our captain brought us an appalling wire from New York. Papa had died of a stroke.

On the long trip home on *The Osprey* I remained most of the time shut up in my cabin, at first in a state of near shock. I had little doubt that Papa's stroke had in part been brought on by a fit of gargantuan rage at one of the saucier of those newspaper reports. If these were not directly attributable to my actions, they were indirectly so, and I had to face the grisly fact that I might have been guilty of a kind of patricide. I had also to face the bleak realization that, despite his sternness and irascibility, I had loved my father. And what was even harder to bear was my new strong feeling that he had loved me—that I had very likely been the only person in the world whom he *had* loved.

Grandpa Thorn's favoritism may have been a kind of pose, the lovable old tycoon's fondness for a dear little girl, but Papa's was true. Oh, I could see that now! Mama had faintly bored him; Otto had alienated him; and my sisters' frivolity had exasperated him; but he had found me worthy of the brilliant life with Walter that he had so carefully and, I now supposed, lovingly planned. He had wanted me to have the success that he had never attained, which was why he had rejected Miles so fiercely and why he had retrieved Walter from his broken romance with Beatrice.

When we arrived in New York, I saw Miles among the waiting crowd at the dock, but I wouldn't speak to him, nor would I see him when he called later at the house.

After the long funeral and the sober sight of the big clan all in black, life for my mother and siblings began slowly to resume its normal course. Mama, for the rest of her long life, believed with me that Papa's demise had been caused by the newspapers, but I don't think she ever held it against me. He had been a mildly disturbing element in the placid silence of her card-playing, card-leaving existence. Serenity now could reign. Otto, deprived of his old grudge, had to content himself by muttering to me, "I don't know if there's a hell, but if there is, he's surely in it." And the effect of Papa's steely control of his female offspring was easily cast off by my sisters. I was the only member of the family, and certainly the only one of Grandpa's posterity, to be strongly affected.

It was as if Papa had rung down a heavy curtain, like the big red one we faced at the opera, or the drab asbestos one that preceded it, on any future that I may have dreamed of having with Miles. I could not face the imagined prospect, no matter how fanciful or superstitious, of his rising from the dead—or from Otto's hell—to blast me for defying the prohibition for which, it gruesomely struck me, he had died to prescribe. I could not so turn him into a futility, even though Otto did not hesitate to suggest that only by doing so could I liberate myself and live. But was Otto much freer? He was to die at thirty-five from an overdose of morphine, whether taken accidentally or on purpose we never knew.

So I gave up Miles. And I was not being weak-minded. I knew, perfectly well, that Miles would have been a poor husband. I had always known it. It was indeed perhaps the strongest of his attractions, that he failed so completely to fit into the world of the Thorns except as a jester or clown. And I? Had I not seen it as my doom that I was too natural a fit not to make a life of fitness? We would have been an ill-fated match.

It is all very well for Lily to maintain, as she still does, that Miles might have made something of his life, married to me. But I doubt if men who need a woman to make a success of their lives ever do. Certainly Walter had no such need. And Lily herself married a man of great steadiness and common sense; it was *he* who helped *her* to make a success of her life. While poor Miles failed in everything he did. When, twenty years later, having gone into a business of importing silk ties and scarves from Cambodia, he never returned from one of his expeditions into jungle territory, he left an estate of nothing but debts. I found it lugubriously fascinating that his jungle tracks had been followed into a copse of trees with nothing leading out, so that the two survivors of his trek had theorized that he may have been attacked, strangled and consumed by a giant python. It would have been like the god Dionysus, of whom he reminded me, to have left no trace of his exit. If these reflections sound cold, I remind myself that I had not seen him in two decades.

Wintie Tillinghast was not the person who decided me to marry Walter, but it was in a conversation with him that I came to that conclusion. He had made a condolence call at the house, and I received him alone. Wintie was the perfect confidant, because he was so little concerned with anything but form. Talking to him could be a kind of confessional. Though stiff, he was kind.

"Do you know what is really odd about me?" I asked. "It's my feeling that if I had had a real romance with Miles, if I had felt for him what Juliet felt for her Romeo, I shouldn't have minded so much what it did to Papa. It would have been worth it, in a horrible way. But to have killed him over someone I wouldn't have married anyway seems to call for expiation."

"And Walter will be that?"

"Yes, don't you see it?"

"No, Agnes, I do not."

But I was hardly listening. What I had said was a monologue. And life with Walter turned out to be exactly what Papa had wanted for me. I had some fascinating times; I saw much of the world; I met all kinds of famous people. And I did my part, too, my small part. And my money, too, my small fraction of the Thorn millions, was quite enough to take financial concerns off Walter's busy mind and to maintain us in a style befitting his importance. Was it all worth it? To know that I'd have to know what a different life would have brought me, and that, fortunately, is something we can never know.

Harry's Brother

AT LEAST they don't laugh at me anymore. Oh, of course, I know that many people feel it's better to be laughed at than despised, but they haven't been laughed at all their lives as I have. As far back as the years immediately preceding the Great War —the first one, I mean, when I was a boy at the Bovee School on Fifth Avenue and Sixty-fourth Street, in 1911 and 1912— my egg-shaped head and goggly eyes, my lisp and roly-poly torso aroused sniffs and sneers. And even at home, in our tall, narrow graystone house on East Seventieth Street, I was aware that the opaque eyes of my erect and awesomely well-dressed father and the more brooding ones of my plain but nobly profiled mother, and the sometimes tolerant ones of my cheerful but easily irritated Irish nurse, tended to glance past me to the romping jovial figure of my younger (by only a year) brother, Harry—the ever-adored Harry. And let me set down right here that Harry was always nice to me. Yes, Harry was lovely to me. He was the only person, I sometimes think, who was.

Harry found everything to his taste: our parents loving and life congenial. I did not. My father, Charles Augustus Pierce, an eminent figure at the New York bar (in a day when birth and superior airs almost made up for minor deficiencies in talent), an eloquent and unheeded advocate of political reform, and my serious, high-minded mother, noted for her night classes in poetry for female telephone operators, had the peculiar aptitude, common to many of the upper class of their day, of making a comfortable life uncomfortable. There was always a principle to be evoked whenever a pleasure loomed. If we traveled as a family in Europe, for example, the big rented Daimler or Panhard limousine had to be stopped on the outskirts of any town visited so that we could trudge our weary way through the *banlieue* to the luxury hotel where we were to stay and be edified by the reminder that the comfort in store for us was not shared by all. But if Harry complained, however insincerely, of a sore foot or headache, the limousine would whisk him on to our hostelry.

I never had to be told of the precariousness of our so-called privileges. The high fence around the campus of the New England boarding school to which I was sent after Bovee was as instrumental in keeping the enemy in as in keeping him out, and I was constantly reminded by jeers and sometimes blows that my speech was affected, my walk mincing and my general appearance that of a sissy. I could only try to counter this by concentrating on my studies and achieving a high academic status, but unfortunately I was living in a milieu, both at school and later at college, where good grades were a detriment in the cultivation of popularity.

Harry's grades, of course, were abysmal. But he was loved by any group in which he happened to find himself, though neither particularly handsome—short, if muscular, with craggy features and tousled blond hair—nor particularly athletic, except in boxing. The explanation of his popularity had to be in the extraordinary charm of the good will and good-natured laughter that radiated from him and seemed to puncture the sullenest or moodiest skin. Harry defied the world to pout. He would give away his last nickel to a beggar, but he would give away yours too, if you let it slip into his hands. He had little sense of private property, which, of course, was to lead to his doom. He was never able to earn a living, but felt passionately that he—and everyone else—was entitled to live.

He had our parents completely under his thumb. They seemed to feel that God had made up to them for his first mistake in me, Charles, Jr., with this subsequent rectification. And when Harry came home in 1919 after the war, where he had first been an ambulance driver and later a second lieutenant at the front, with a Silver Star for gallantry in action, these two old patriots believed that their role in life was to support and back up their hero in his every venture. It was to cost them dearly. But would they listen to me, who through no fault of my own, had been rejected by the armed forces for deficient eyesight? Need I answer the question?

Harry's business ventures—an oater movie, a small yacht-rental company, a silver mine and ultimately a waxwork museum—were all disasters and made disastrous holes in the family capital. But Father felt that his darling could not be let down, and after his death Mother was worse. Nor were Harry's three marriages more successful. The first was to a gold-digging Hollywood starlet who left him for a bag of gold—and with a bag of gold. The second was to a genial and beautiful society heiress, and their ten-year union was a romp in which each beautifully tolerated the affairs of the other. When she left Harry for an obvious gigolo with whom she was unashamedly infatuated, Harry not only refused a penny of the big settlement that she cheerfully offered him but gave her a great bash of an engagement party! "A *mari complaisant* can be a gentleman," he observed when I protested that he should accept some reparation for what she had wildly spent of his money, "but a paid *mari complaisant* can only be a cad." His third wife, an unexpectedly dear little brown thing, poor as a church mouse, whom he adored, died in giving birth to a stillborn babe, the sole issue of his three matrimonial ventures, and he mourned her grievously. "What does it tell you about me, Chas, that I've caused the death of the only person I've ever loved more than myself? I must have the evil eye. Why don't people avoid me?"

Because they couldn't. Could I? Harry never gave up trying to "make a gentleman" of me, or what people might consider a gentleman. He introduced me to girls, nice girls, carefully selected by him, who would not be too bold or too flashy to put me off, who might be content to become the friendly if not adoring spouse of such a respectable and providing mate as I might prove. All in vain. I was not aroused. Then he took me to an expensive brothel, where he had coached one of the gentler inmates on how to lure me without alarming me. It didn't work. At last he decided that he had better accept me as neuter and train me to look as well as I could in that role.

"Be a permanent bachelor, if that's what you want, old boy," he told me with a clap on the shoulder, "but be a great one. Acquire the reputation of being a 'character.' We'll get you dressed up in the finest dark suits and white stiff collars—no color except for a gorgeous Charvet tie. You must become known as punctual, exact, a bit on the pompous side. Don't be afraid to look shocked at modern slang and dirty talk. Go in for mens' clubs. Their committee chairmanships are always available to anyone who's willing to do the work, and you'll find yourself running each place in no time. And when people start saying, 'God broke the mold after he created Charley Pierce,' you'll know you've made the grade!"

And do you know, he was right? Between us we created the Charles Pierce who has for years been the secretary-treasurer of the Hone Club and who is known as the punctilious and exacting *éminence grise* behind the popular and easygoing president of that venerable institution, and an active vice-president of the Sons of the American Revolution. People may have still laughed at me, but their laughter was friendlier, and Harry's was the loudest and friendliest of all.

My rise from a clerk in the Standard Loan and Trust Company to that of senior trust officer seemed somehow inevitably wedded to my rise to a highly respected niche in Manhattan mens' club life and Knickerbocker society. I also found myself in a position to pay Harry back for his kindness to me by rectifying some of the damage he had done to the family finances. When I discovered that Father, clinging in his old age, to the starchy habits of old-time lawyers in having no social contact with the less savory of the firm's clients, was losing much of his percentage of its profits to greedy younger partners who failed to recognize the kudos that Father's small civic reputation had brought to them, I was able to arrange not only that my bank should continue to give its substantial legal business to them (the use of another law firm had been strenuously urged by the officers of another bank with which we had merged) but that Father's name should be kept in the firm's books as the partner in charge. And after his death I persuaded

Mother to place all of her much-diminished assets in a trust, with my bank and myself as trustees. At the last moment she insisted that Harry, from whose importunities I was, of course, protecting her, should be a third trustee, and I acceded to her wish, confident that the bank and I could always outvote him if necessary and perfectly willing that he should get the commissions that I would gladly renounce.

Was there hidden envy of or hostility to Harry in my making up for his depredations? Was it intensified by our parents' stubborn refusal to see in what I did for them anything more than my duty, while the smallest favor conveyed by Harry was greeted with hugs? At any rate I must have been sorely tried.

Harry's last venture was the waxwork museum, with which he hoped to rival Madame Tussaud's in London. But it was from the beginning a small and somewhat tawdry affair, based on one floor of a loft building in Chelsea with dioramas of scenes from New York City history, financed insufficiently by a rich army friend. (His pre-war pals were disillusioned, at least with his businesses.) I had put up a small sum and vowed that was all.

World War II was in its closing weeks, and Harry, who had served as lieutenant colonel on MacArthur's staff in Australia but had been released from duty after a mild heart attack, had had a year to develop his new project. I found Mother, who had welcomed old age as an overdue admirer, gaunt, bent over and beshawled before the big pasteboard on which she had affixed the newspaper clippings of the gallant war doings of younger friends and relations around a large central photograph of Harry receiving his honorable discharge from the hands of the great liberator of the Philippines. The contrast between the pictured uniforms and my habitual black made me feel like a minor minister of state having a wartime conference with his august sovereign. I almost wondered whether I should take a seat before I was bidden.

"Will Harry have a waxwork of General MacArthur in his museum?" I asked, as little sarcastically as I could.

"Why not?" Mother demanded indignantly, picking up at once such sarcasm as appeared. "There might be a wonderful one of his wading ashore on the beach of Leyte. It ill becomes those who have stayed at home to sneer, Charles."

"Nor had I any intention of doing so, Mother. But I suppose it wasn't to discuss subjects for Harry's dioramas that you sent for me."

"Not at all. I am afraid that Harry is going to need a substantial sum of money to save his museum from bankruptcy."

"And how can he expect to raise that? No bank will look at him, as we know, and even this latest of his army friends must have seen the writing on the wall."

"You're very harsh on the subject of your brother's finances, Charles. Not everyone has had the good fortune that has favored you. And I wonder that it doesn't occur to you that those men who were exempted from military duty in two world wars may have incurred the obligation to come to the aid of those who served their country in the battlefield."

I could almost admire my intrepid parent for scorning to be anything but undiplomatic. "It was not my fault that the army rejected me. And I have always been ready to assist Harry in his personal needs, though not in his business enterprises, except for a token contribution. If Harry needs money to pay his household bills, he knows he can send them to me. I never give him cash, because I know what he'll do with it."

"But that's so insulting, Charles!"

"It's based on painful experience. Anyway, to anticipate your request, I am not prepared to give him a cent for his waxworks."

"I am not asking you to do that," Mother retorted with considerable hauteur. "I know you too well, Charles. What I am suggesting—or rather what I am requesting—is that you advance Harry the hundred thousand dollars that he needs from my trust."

I bit my lip in surprise. Such a sum was a small fortune in 1945. "It can't be done. It's out of the question."

"What do you mean, it can't be done?"

"Correction. I mean it won't be done."

"Does the trust deed not give the trustees the power to invade principal?"

"For your benefit. Not for Harry's."

"But you wouldn't be giving the money to Harry! You'd be giving it to me first, of course, if you must be technical about it. And I'd be directing you to pay it to Harry. Can't I do what I wish with my own?"

"When it's your own, yes. But your fiduciaries must use their discretion in distributing capital for your benefit. And two of your three trustees, the bank and I, will hardly find it discreet to strip the fund, on which you none too lavishly exist, for a waxwork museum."

"But it might kill me if Harry fails! Isn't that such an emergency as the trust might call for? Think of all that poor boy has been through, with his heart trouble and losing that darling little wife and child and not being able to finish the war in the company of his great idol, the general!"

I couldn't help wondering what horrors could befall me that would "kill," or even grievously upset, my wonderful mother. The reflection would have helped to tighten, if tightening were needed, my resolution never to exercise that trust power except for the direst emergency affecting the life tenant. My reply perhaps sounded pontifical, but an undervalued son must have some compensation.

"We must pray then that the refusal of your fiduciaries to stretch the exercise of their power beyond the limits prescribed by law will not have the dire effect on the income beneficiary that you so dismally predict."

"Oh, Charles, you're impossible."

"It is not I who am that, Mother. It is what you ask of me."

"Leave me alone. Go away."

Which I was glad enough to do.

I did not hear of the matter for another month, and then it was only indirectly. Indirectly but fatally. At the bank one morning when I was getting ready to depart for my lunch club, Ray Burnside, the fussy but earnest diminutive assistant trust officer in charge of Mother's affairs, faced me across my desk with a pale countenance drawn with apprehension. It appeared that a hundred thousand dollars worth of U.S. Treasury notes were missing from her trust.

"You mean stolen?" I asked, gaping.

"No, no. At least I dare not think so. You will remember that we had agreed to sell them, and your brother asked me to deliver them to him so that he could use his own broker."

I felt at once sick. "You shouldn't have done that. You should have come to me."

"But after all, he is a trustee."

"Even so. How long have the notes been gone?"

"Three weeks. I've telephoned your brother several times to ask whether he's sold them and, if so, where the proceeds are. He keeps putting me off and insisting on more time. Says it's not a good market to sell in, which is ridiculous, of course, and gives me all sorts of odd excuses. If you can't get him to give us back the notes or the money, Charles, I'll have to go to the big boss."

I thought for a moment and then nodded. "Give me till tomorrow. I'll take care of it."

What made me so immediately sure that Harry had embezzled the money? What right had I to accuse, even in my mind alone, my amiable brother of a crime, when he had never been known to commit one? It may have been because I had come to my limit in believing in a universe that was so consistently perverse as to favor Harry with everyone's smiles and love and me with their sniggers and reluctant respect. There had to be somewhere a stop; Harry had to have his comeuppance. And wasn't the horrid thrill that seemed to trickle through my being one of an odious satisfaction? Wasn't it an essential part of the creature I had been made? And, after all, I hadn't made myself, had I? I could be at fault only if I acted on it.

I telephoned Harry to say that I was coming over to his museum to ask about the notes, and he replied, quite without agitation, that he would meet me in the main gallery. This long dark chamber was empty when I arrived, although the place was open to the public. It contained a dozen dioramas of city history, some moderately amusing, such as J. P. Morgan immersed in a game of solitaire as he awaits the answer to his proposition of how to bolster a crashing stock market from the grim group of bankers gathered around him, or the dapper figure of Mayor Jimmy Walker skipping down the steps of City Hall with a gorgeous flapper on his arm. I was contemplating the representation of Diana Vreeland at her desk in the office of the editor of *Vogue* when a voice from behind me sounded suddenly in my ear.

"That is not a waxwork. That is Diana herself. She comes every day in her lunch hour and poses. Don't you love it?"

Of course, it was Harry, but for a moment I almost believed him. As a joker, he could be amazingly dead pan.

"Can you never be serious?" I asked with a sigh. "You know why I've come."

"Aren't trusts too serious to be taken seriously? Think of what a wonderful diorama we could make of you and Mr. Burnside when you discovered the missing notes. Or rather when you didn't discover the missing notes."

I looked about in search of a more fitting place for our talk. But what could be more private than the empty gallery? There was a bench in the center, and we moved to it.

"Burnside is behaving perfectly well," I told him. "He hasn't made any insinuations. He simply wants the notes or the proceeds of their sale deposited in the bank tomorrow. Or he will go to our president. It's the only thing he can do."

"And the president will go to the cops?"

"He will go, unless I can give him an acceptable explanation, to the district attorney. It's the only thing *he* can do."

"It would be an even better diorama with which to close my ill-fated museum! Harry Pierce in a striped suit!"

"Harry, for God's sake, what have you done with those notes?"

Harry was as calm and reflective as if I had asked him

about an ordinary business transaction. "Well, I had only a limited time, three weeks as it turns out, to make the hundred gees double themselves so that I'd be able to save my museum and put the money back in the bank. There was just one way to do that, and that was by gambling. I had a glorious week in Las Vegas. At one point I was up to a hundred and eighty thousand. And then I lost it all."

"All of it? I thought that only happened in French nineteenth-century novels!"

"Maybe that's where I belong. I haven't a friend in the world who would lend me the money now. I'd have to tell them why, and then they'd drop me like a hot potato."

"Why would you have to tell them?"

"Because they're friends, damn it all! I should have told Mother, but she said you'd never invade the trust, so there was no point."

"I guess that leaves me."

"No, Chas! Never!"

"It won't bust me. Don't worry."

Harry was suddenly deeply earnest. He turned to face me and grasped my shoulders. "You can't do it. Not now that you know what I've done. You'd be compounding a crime."

"Oh, bosh. No one need know."

"Burnside would know."

"I can take care of Burnside."

"But you'd be in his hands. If ever he needed you to back his promotion. No, Chas, I can't accept that."

"Leave the details to me, Harry."

He jumped to his feet, more worked up than I had ever seen him. "I absolutely forbid it! All your life you've been the good boy and I've been the bad. And what have you got for it?

Precious little. Even from Father and Mother. Even after you made up to them for all the losses I'd caused. Oh, I knew about all that; yes I did! And now you want to turn yourself into a crook to save a crook. Well, I won't have it! If there's one decent thing I can do now, I'm going to do it. Don't stand in my way, Chas. I mean it!"

"But, Harry," I cried, aghast, "you'll go to jail!"

"And tell me, dear brother, isn't that where I belong?"

Harry went to the penitentiary for two years, and I eventually made up the loss to Mother's trust out of my own pocket. But did I get any credit for that? Far from it. She and plenty of others among the family and friends excoriated me for not doing it in time to save him, and when Harry wrote to her that he had forbidden me to compound his crime, the universal attitude was that I should have saved him in spite of himself and that my reaching for the excuse of a breach of law, which would have never been discovered or, if it had, probably been condoned, was a mere blind to hide my jealousy and resentment of my popular and beloved sibling. And they may have been right, too, in the funny way that people have of being right when they attribute nasty motives to one. For had I not been sure that Harry would reject my offer to save him, and didn't that give me the excuse I may have consciously or unconsciously needed to throw him to the dogs?

When Harry's term was over, after only sixteen months because of model prison behavior, he was greeted at his club with a huge and hearty "coming-out" party, to which I was not invited. But, as I have said, people don't laugh at me anymore. And that's something.

Entre Deux Guerres

The Marriage Broker

THE THING THAT intrigues me most about my mother-in-law's family—almost as much as it irritates me, but never quite, oh no!—is the way they silently, and yet so audibly, disapprove of what they reluctantly concede to be my charm, a quality notably lacking in all of them, with the exception of my husband and two children, and at the same time expect me to use this sole asset of mine (if such it be) to pull them out of the social and financial holes into which they ever more deeply sink. And there we were, in 1937, the year of which I am writing, incurably wed to our expensive tastes and just as incurably lacking what used to be a moderately comfortable little family fortune.

Grinnell Scott, my lord but no longer my master (I have had to take up the reins of management), may still be one of the most beloved and popular sportsmen on the Northeastern Seaboard, a long-term president of the New York Golf and Tennis Club and a squash racquets champion at age fifty-five. But with a genial smile and shrug of his shoulders he leaves all business matters to me, droning, in his pleasant whine, "But, Katie, sweet, you always got high school marks, and you know I could never add two and two." Well, I've done my best, but I can't perform the miracle of the loaves and fishes, and I've had to rent our house in Manhattan and park my little family the year round in our shingle villa in Bar Harbor, inadequately heated for a Maine winter, where we can gaze out the windows at the cold gray Atlantic and envy our departed summer neighbors, tucked away cozily in their southern homes.

But I must say about Grinnell and the children that although they left the decisions to me, they never complained. Grinnell insisted that cross-country skiing, which he can do in Maine, was the sport in which he had always wished to indulge, and the twins, Elfrida and Damon, now thirty and cheerfully unemployed, were equally content, Elfrida with her watercolors and Damon with the opportunity to get on with that novel he was always going to write.

My mother-in-law, typically, managed to keep her New York apartment open so that she was spared the rigor of Maine winters. Much later, on her demise, we learned that she had done it by spending all the capital that might have come to my children. Really, she and Grinnell's maiden sisters were incomparable. Serene in their smugness and fatuity, confident that their Colonial blood was envied by all (actually, my family was much better) and proud of what they called the Scott "pluck" (they would pale at the sight of a cockroach), they counted on me to ingratiate myself with the new rich of Bar Harbor, when summer came, and marry off Elfrida and Damon to advantage. But would they help? Heavens, no! They would not lower themselves to meet the newcomers and did not hesitate to look down on me for being able to do the job on which they counted but the mechanics of which they despised—and congratulated themselves for despising! For would a lady, a real lady, care as I had to care about clothes and looks and ingratiating manners? Of course not!

And I must admit that they are not wholly incorrect in their judgment of me. I *do* use people. My only real resentment of my in-laws is that they expect to profit from the dirty water into which they decline to stick a finger. It is I who must handle the new rich with whom they don't care to associate. And, of course, I have learned how to do that. I am well aware of how social climbers make use of summer resorts, which represent the soft underbelly of the old guard. In their hometowns —Boston, New York, Philadelphia—the established families are more or less secure in their guarded citadels: the clubs, the private schools, the subscription dances, even some of the major charities. But at a watering place like Newport, Bar Harbor or Southampton the new tycoon (provided he is not too repellently vulgar, as a surprising number are) can attract the children of the old guard to play with his children by offering them the use of yachts, fast foreign cars, well-kept tennis courts and other luxuries, and once the younger generation has been lured in, the parents are almost bound to call, and the fortifications are breached. Marriages between the old and new soon guarantee total acceptance, and the battle is won.

But there are pitfalls for those who, like myself, are bent on hastening the process. A member of the old guard must not surrender too quickly; it will be assumed that he or she is a phoney, not the real thing. And, secondly, the friendship that you finally offer a newcomer must be sincere. After all, these people, even if they need polish, are not stupid. They wouldn't have made their millions if they were. And, like other people, they want to be loved. And this is not always impossible. Take Mrs. Oscar Gleason, my prize capture, widow of the rubber tycoon whose mammoth fortune was rumored to be derived in good part from contraceptives. I admired and respected this grave and regal dowager from the beginning and was genuinely amused, as were so many others, by her six handsome if rather madcap children. Indeed, I think I can say truly that I came to love that family.

My own family (as opposed to my in-laws) proved useful allies. Good-natured and essentially democratic, my husband and son and daughter made friends easily with everyone on the island. In fact, I doubt that Grinnell made any distinction in his mind between the old stock and the new. His athletic prowess and easygoing manner shed a beam of light about him, and the business moguls could admire his muscle and enjoy his sometimes naïve amiability without envying his brain. It rather fascinated them that he had never worked, and his explanation of this was much repeated at the swimming club. He had worked, he told them, for a year after his graduation from Harvard, as a customers' man in a Wall Street brokerage house, but when he discovered that he and his chauffeur had the same salary, he decided to drive himself and be free of toil. This, I may say, was typical of Grinnell. He never read a book, but he wrote one, a short collection of fishing stories, and had it privately and too expensively published, with the placating dedication "to Kate, my companion in the adventure of life." One could forgive him anything, even a bromide. And one always did.

Elfrida was a lovely but passive young woman, perfectly content to be idle, except when painting her mild little pictures, and oddly indifferent to masculine attention. There was not much chance of lassoing a young heir for her, but I knew that if I got an heiress for Damon, he would always look after his twin. Damon was my ace of trumps. Everyone loved him.

He was slight but beautifully built, with dark eyes and hair, romantically good-looking and a fine athlete, though nothing like his father. The few things that he consented to do he did well—tennis, golf and bridge—but he was regrettably lazy and spent hours in the summer stretched out on the porch, acquiring a perfect tan. He appeared to have no ambition and seemed perfectly happy to depend on the small trust fund he had inherited from his grandfather to guard him from industry. Although he lived with me, he did not live on me, insisting that I take a good half of his small income for his maintenance. That was like him.

The great thing about Damon was his character. He was the essence of amiability and kindness to everyone, and especially to me. He and I discussed everything that I could not discuss with his dear but easily distracted father; we thought alike and felt alike and laughed alike. I guess it's sufficiently obvious that Damon was the love of my life.

There had been times, of course, when I tried to persuade him to work, but there was a stubbornness in his quiet insistence on a life of temperate hedonism that I at last came to realize I was not going to overcome. It was I who would have to arrange for his future; nobody else would do it, least of all himself. He had, as I say, his own small means, but if I should die, and my heart is not strong, he would give it to his father and sister whenever they needed it, which would be often. And even if they didn't, it was not enough for him to marry on, and I couldn't bear the idea of his never having a family of his own. Needless to say there were plenty of girls in Bar Harbor who had fallen in love with him, but so far he seemed to have avoided any serious entanglement. There was one woman with whom he enjoyed a deep and lasting friendship, but she was his slightly older first cousin, my niece Leila Bryce, a bright and attractive woman, a Catholic convert who had found herself locked into a miserable marriage with a dissolute and faithless husband from whom she was now separated. I am sure that there were people who raised their eyebrows at Damon and Leila's long intimacy, but he always implied that she was simply another sister to him.

No, if Damon was to marry, it would have to be to an heiress, and as there was not a mercenary bone in his body, it would be up to me to find one for him. Marjorie Gleason was an almost too obvious choice; she was the oldest, prettiest and most lively of my friend Florence's brood and a devoted friend of Damon's. They had even won the swimming club's bridge tournament as partners.

As I have said, I did not consider Damon's friendship with my niece Leila an impediment to my project, but to be sure there were no ambushes lurking in those woods, I put it before her one morning at the swimming club. Leila had come out of the pool and joined me on a stone bench by the water, pulling off her rubber cap and shaking her head to fluff out her lovely blond hair. I admired her glistening wet body, her handsome tanned features and her sympathetic brown eyes, regretting as always that this fine woman, so svelte and youthful-looking at thirty-five, should have tied herself up to the wrong man.

"You know, Aunt Kate, I've had the same idea!" she responded with what certainly sounded like sincerity. "It's high time that Damon got married, and Marjorie Gleason is just the girl he needs. And I've a hunch it won't be too hard to pull off. I'm pretty sure she has a crush on him. But remember, Auntie, don't push too hard! We all have a tendency to shy away from any match Mama favors. Maybe a few nice remarks about Marjorie, well placed, will be enough."

"Oh, I think Damon's natural inertia will need more than that. But don't worry; I'll be tactful."

Leila looked not so sure of this, but she turned to another aspect of the match. "If it should really happen, it might be the making of him. For to be known as the idle mate of an heiress, who has contributed only his good looks and charm to the union, will be galling to Damon. It may convince him to get off his ass and make something of himself!"

Leila had always been a frank talker, but I now thought that she was too frank. "I agree that it may give him a new sense of direction," I retorted, somewhat dryly.

"At any rate, there's nothing to lose, for he couldn't do less than he's doing now."

"You're hard on him, Leila."

"Because I love him, Aunt Kate!"

This reassured me. Would she have used the word if she loved him in a romantic way?

But there was still a hitch. The remarkable thing about the Gleason children was that they all drank. Oh, they were handsome and healthy and happy and fun-loving and rich, but they still drank. Why? Was it just high spirits? And would it pass away when they married and settled down?

It so happened that this very question was put to me by their mother, Florence Gleason herself, in the first conversation I had with her after my resolution to open a campaign in favor of a Damon-Marjorie marriage. Needless to say, it was not I who introduced the subject. I was not so unsubtle. My plan was first of all to clear my son of any suspicion of mercenary motives—the perennial bugbear of both old and new rich—and to do so before mention was made of his marriage to anyone. But Florence forced me to alter my plan of attack. Fortunately, I am quick-witted.

We met that day in the center of Bar Harbor's social life: the umbrella tables on the lawn of the swimming club, looking down on the long blue pool filled with brown youthful bodies. But these did not belong to the rulers of the scene. The rulers were their mothers and grandmothers, much less brown and certainly not youthful but splendidly and colorfully attired, who gathered at noon at the umbrella tables to signal to the red-coated waiters to bring them the first cocktail of the day. A brilliant sky, a sparkling sea, dotted with white sails, and a range beyond the encompassing village of great green hills aspiring to be mountains formed the backdrop to these ladies' spirited analyses of the doings and undoings of yesterday. I used to claim that it was impossible to read the newspaper in Bar Harbor. The big cities, with their angry headlines and toiling husbands, were out of sight and out of mind; we lived in a utopia of smiles and thoughtlessness.

Coming down the steps of the clubhouse that morning to the lawn, I spied Florence Gleason not at her usual table but sitting alone at a corner one, as ladies did when expecting a guest who was not of their regular circle. She beckoned to me, however, and I crossed the lawn to join her.

Florence was tall and gaunt, with great sad eyes and a lined, melancholy countenance. She was dressed in perpetual mourning for a long-dead husband—a spotless white dress with a few black trimmings. She always gave me the curious impression of one who constituted a kind of detached audience to the drama of her life and that of her different and rambunctious offspring. It was not that she wasn't interested in such dramas; she was touched, even moved, but you felt that she had seen the play before and had no control over its outcome. She took her perquisites for granted—the huge stone villa, the yacht and all the shining cars—seeming mildly to protest that she had never sought them.

"I have something to ask you, Kate," she began. "But first let me order you a drink." She beckoned to a waiter.

"Is the sun over the yardarm? Not yet, I see. It must be a serious question."

"Well, as it's about drinking, a drink may be in order. As you are doubtless aware, my children all imbibe. And rather too freely, I fear."

"Oh well, they're young and full of spirits."

"That is indeed what they're full of."

"I didn't mean a pun, Florence."

"And if you did, there's no harm in it. But here's the point. Marjorie, who's the oldest and should set an example to the others, is the worst of all. And I'm afraid she's getting worse. She has a very hard head and carries it well, but think what it must be doing to her liver! I was wondering if your Damon could help her."

This certainly startled me. I had to play for time. "How do you mean?"

"All my children love Damon. He has a wonderful gift with people. And he strikes me as that rare sort of man who is capable of real friendship with a woman."

"A platonic one? That's not always considered a compliment, you know. To the man or the woman."

"Oh, Kate, you know I mean nothing like that. Your

Damon is as manly as anyone. And for that matter, isn't he taken up with that lovely niece of yours? Forgive me, dear, but one can't help hearing what people say."

I began to feel the fates were against me. "There's nothing in that! They're like brother and sister!"

"Anyway, he's much more *sympathique* than Marjorie's other men friends. He could talk to her about her drinking without arousing her resentment. Which I have certainly been unable to do."

I thought now that I could see my way. "Well, I can certainly talk to him about it." And then I smiled, as if to end on a lighter note. "And in case you have any worry about such an increase in their intimacy affecting the platonic nature of their friendship, I can tell you that Damon has always sworn he'd die the loneliest old bachelor in the world rather than marry an heiress."

"Oh?" There was a distinct chill in Florence's tone.

"He says that the man who marries money earns it. Of course, that has nothing to do with your Marjorie, who is adorable and could marry any boy on the island she wished."

"Except, I gather, your Damon. Well, it's just as well, I guess. I'd have a hard time selling him to the Gleason trustees."

It was my turn to feel a chill. "Why would you have a hard time?"

"Well, you know how those people are. Damon is a fine young man—there's not a spot on him, I'm sure—but he doesn't have the things trustees expect. A steady job or a future or, apparently, the desire for one."

I exploded. "The day Damon settles down to something—and he will, mind you—he will surprise you. He has a first-class mind and a golden character. And the girl who marries him will have a first-class husband, one who will love her and support her and guide her and cherish her all the days of her life! A fat lot your trustees know about that!"

My temper had accomplished what my scheming had not. Florence sat silent, like one transfixed. And I had suddenly a picture, crystal clear, of what was going through her mind. She was having a vision of what such a husband, with time on his hands, time to devote to a bibulous spouse, might do for her wayward daughter. And what did she care about the Gleason trustees, anyway? Could she not bend them to her wishes?

"Is Damon really so averse to an heiress?" she asked at last.

"Who knows? Love conquers all, they say."

"Do you know what else they say, Kate? They say that *you* are the real cause that Damon stays single. That you make him much too comfortable at home for him to think of leaving."

"*Do* they say so?"

"My dear, the best thing in the world for that young man might be for you to kick him out of the nest!"

"And if I do that, Florence, what will you do for me?"

"What would you like me to do?"

"Give the Gleason trustees a good kick in the pants!"

She stared at me for a moment and then laughed. At which point I suggested that we join our usual group, who were gathering at the center table. I had accomplished a miracle, and I knew that I must avoid the danger of going too far.

That same day after dinner I had a long and serious talk with Damon. Perhaps it would be more accurate to call it a monologue, for I certainly spoke twenty words to his one. I outlined our grim financial situation and, should I die, the fix that he would be in without my capable hands to manage his father and sister, and with the income of his little trust at the mercy of his own generosity, which bordered on weakness. I expounded on the virtues of Marjorie Gleason and the joys of paternity and family life, and I took it upon myself to predict that, satisfied with a loving spouse, the heiress would turn from the pleasures of the bottle to those of the domestic hearth.

"You're taking a lot for granted, Mumsy," was his first dry rejoinder, when I had paused to take a breath. "What makes you so sure that I'd be such an ideal husband, particularly for a girl who can pick and choose among the many aspirants who dog her steps?"

"You've been the best of sons," I affirmed stoutly. "And the best of friends to many. Why shouldn't you be the best of husbands?"

"I noticed you never mentioned love."

I hesitated. But wouldn't that long, calm, clear gaze with which he now fixed me win any woman's heart? "Kindness—and your heart is full of that, my boy—can be as good as love."

"And would Marjorie's kindness—assuming she has as much as you say I have—be enough for me?"

"Marjorie has more than kindness for you, and you know it! Haven't I seen you together? The girl is dippy about you. Maybe it's your failure to respond that's making her drink more."

I could see he didn't like this. He didn't like it at all. "More? How do you know she's drinking more?"

"Her mother told me."

"You mean I should marry her to get her off the booze?"

"Well, it would be a Christian reason. To add to all the other good ones."

"And am I such a good Christian?"

"Ethically, yes. And Marjorie's not the only person you'd be doing it for."

"Oh, I see that. I'd be doing it for you, too."

"Oh, it would make me so happy, my dear! It would make up for everything else that's gone wrong in my life!"

A sudden light of pain in his eyes flashed on me. "Oh, Ma, you make things very hard."

With which he rose and abruptly left me. I knew better than to follow him or to allude to the subject again. I had planted the seed; I could let it grow on its own.

For a couple of weeks I noticed no alteration in his conduct. He continued to frequent the Gleasons' villa, where some kind of social gathering was almost always taking place, but, then, he had long been a regular guest there. However, as the season advanced and autumn approached, I was glad to note that he was starting to see Marjorie apart from her family, taking her to the movies or to hikes on our "mountains," as we called them, and on three occasions to meals at our house. On one such day, at noon before lunch, she and I were sitting on the veranda watching my husband and Damon playing croquet on the lawn below. Annie, my old waitress-cook, had earlier brought her a cocktail, and now Marjorie held up the empty glass to indicate to my obviously disapproving servitor that she wanted another.

"You don't really want it, do you, dear?" I asked in my mildest tone. "I always think twice before I have a second. Particularly so early in the day."

Marjorie looked at me with frank surprise, and then shook

her head to indicate to Annie a change of mind. She settled her long thin brown body, so much of which was exposed by her scanty white tennis dress, in her chair with the clear intention of taking me up on my cautioning. Her face was oddly attractive, despite being flat and round, her eyes small but piercing. And her self-assurance was supreme, backed by an intelligence too sharp to countenance idle resentment.

"You think I drink too much, Mrs. Scott." It was the simplest statement of fact.

"I think we all do. We should keep an eye on one another."

"Of course, you don't expect me to keep an eye on you. Nor should I think of doing so. But I take your interest as showing that you regard me in a different light from Damon's other girlfriends."

"If you mean that I'm particularly fond of you, you're quite right."

"Thank you. And let me in turn reassure you. The day that I decide to give up my drinking, I will do so. Completely."

"And you will have a very happy life."

"And I am fully aware that you expect that happy life to be shared with your son. It's all right; I find that perfectly natural on a mother's part."

I decided quickly to reply in the same frank note. "May I hope that you share that expectation?"

"You may hope what you please, Mrs. Scott. But let me advise you not to push your son. Whatever he may decide to do, he'll do it better on his own. Let's face the hard fact that you've hardly made much of a success of him so far."

"But he's only thirty!" I cried, stung to the quick.

"Think what Napoleon had done at thirty!"

"You want a Napoleon?"

"No, but I don't want a mother's boy."

The men had finished their match and were about to join us for lunch, and Marjorie and I, as it was to turn out, had had our first and last discussion of alcoholism and marriage. I was on the whole pleased with what she had said. She obviously disliked me, but I wasn't the person I wanted her to marry, and it was quite clear that she would be a strong wife for Damon and that he had only to shape up a bit before putting the question.

It seemed fitting to the unreal quality of the air and sea of our magic isle that the bad news, when it came, should come from one whom I had never known to supply any but the least consequential information: from my impassive and unimaginative daughter, Elfrida. It came one morning when she and I were sitting idly on the veranda, she with a novel and I with my needlepoint, and I chanced to observe, almost half to myself, "Doesn't it show what determined gossips some people are that they have been so fixed in their idea that something was going on between Leila and Damon?"

To my surprise, Elfrida, usually so placid, closed her book smartly. "What on earth makes you say that?"

"Well, isn't it obvious that Leila's pushing Damon as hard as she can into Marjorie's arms?"

"Oh, yes, she's doing that, all right."

"Well, how could she be doing that if she's in love with him herself?"

"It's simple. She wants what's best for him."

"Elfrida, are you implying . . . ?"

"That they're lovers? Of course I am! And have been for

years. As you would know yourself, if you hadn't always worn blinkers about the doings of your favorite child!"

In my shock at this double thunderbolt, I had no time to reflect on its revelation of the bitter sibling rivalry that may have, unknownst to me, dominated the life of my neglected daughter. I had to concentrate desperately on what I was learning about my son. "But no woman could be so selfless as to give up the man she loved to another woman because she thought it best for him!"

"Who says she's giving him up?"

"Elfrida, what are you saying?"

"They'll never give each other up. They'll go right on as they always have."

I gasped. "And Marjorie?"

"Oh, they'll think they can keep it from her; they've kept it from plenty of people. They'd have kept it from me, except Leila had to have one confidante, and she trusted me. You should hear her! She thinks she's like Cathy in *Wuthering Heights*. 'I *am* Damon!' she told me once. What rot!"

So there it was, in the waves dashing on the gray rocks of the coastline, in the golden sunlight, in the deep green of the pine trees, in the gayly colored dresses and painted faces under the umbrella tables at the club and on my own veranda, facing the blue expanse of Frenchman's Bay—the sparkle of evil.

I have always spoken of my quick wits. They had got me into this jam; now they would have to get me out. There would be no use, I knew at once, in challenging Damon with my awareness of his proposed breach of faith. He would deny it to me, to everyone, even to himself. He had the habit, perhaps derived in part from his mental laziness, of seeing each chapter of his deliberately uneventful life as an independent entity, unrelated to any other. Thus, he would have been quite capable of seeing his duty to his mother and his duty to Marjorie and his duty to Leila as things not connected but each to be defined in its own terms. What he did with Leila, therefore, need not have anything to do with Marjorie. Oh, it had to be hidden, of course, but only because other people had strange notions. Did this excuse him or make him worse? I neither knew nor cared. It was up to me to stand between him and the devil or whatever this fetid thing was. He may have been, as Elfrida said, my favorite child; he may indeed have been my favorite person in all the world; but my love for him was far from blind.

I waited up that night until he came home, very late, and insisted that he mix me a nightcap. He was tired but, as always, compliant. I then asked him directly whether he and Marjorie were engaged. Surprised, he said no. Then I asked him whether he had given her any reason to expect a proposal of marriage.

"What's all this about, Ma? Are you trying to hurry me up?"

"Quite the contrary. Please answer my question."

"Well, no, I don't think I have."

"Thank God! I've been making inquiries, as any conscientious mother should. Darling boy, try to forgive me, but I've put you on the wrong track. The general opinion is that Marjorie's drinking problem is not one that she's apt to get over. If you marry her, you'll be taking on a lifetime job."

Damon rose, as was his way when a subject became distasteful, and walked to the foot of the stairs. "I think I'll say good night now. And, Mother, will you please give up your matchmaking? It doesn't do either of us much good."

And with this he left me.

I don't know how he settled things with Marjorie, but if he was true to his usual form, he did nothing. Soon, it became apparent that she and Damon were not going to alter their friendship in any significant way, and a year later she became engaged to a young man with a fortune not larger than the Gleason fortune but equal to Marjorie's fractional interest in it. As Elfrida remarked to me bleakly, she could be sure that she was not being married for her money.

At any rate, the poor girl wasn't to have much of a life, for she died of cirrhosis of the liver three years later. Damon, who was still living at home with me and his father and sister and still supposedly working on his novel (never finished and perhaps never begun) was silent about the tragedy, but that was like him. It was always hard to tell whether his reaction to such news was a feeling too deep to be imparted or mere indifference. Leila was no longer in our picture. She had been reconciled to her husband and moved to California. But one hot summer night in Bar Harbor, when Damon and I were alone in the living room, I reading a novel and he a magazine, I couldn't bear not to discuss poor Marjorie.

"Do you think she may have married her husband on the rebound?"

He did not look up. "Marjorie, do you mean? On the rebound from what?"

"Oh, from her failure to land my handsome son." I tried to make it light and failed.

"What makes you think she tried to land him?"

"I have eyes, haven't I? She found you too preoccupied with your cousin Leila, perhaps."

At this, he threw aside his magazine. "Mother, what are you getting at?"

But if he was going to be angry, so was I. "Well, you were having an affair, weren't you?"

Damon got up, strode to the fireplace and then turned to face me. He had submitted, as he rarely did, to the disagreeable necessity of a serious discussion. "We *had* had an affair, yes," he said flatly. "Does that shock you? Do you think it was incestuous, between first cousins?"

"Oh, no, dear, no. It's just that everything you do is of the greatest interest to me."

"Leila and I always knew where we stood vis-à-vis each other. She was married and, as a good Catholic, would not countenance a divorce. Besides, we agreed that we were too closely related to risk having children. So what was left for us but to have an affair? Which we did, to our great mutual satisfaction. It seemed to me eminently sensible. It still does. Do you disagree?"

"Oh, no, I'm not such a prude. But this affair, my dear, when did it end?"

"I don't remember exactly. Some three or four years ago. When she started to have conscience pangs about her husband and whether or not she should go back to him. Which, of course, ultimately she did."

"That must have been very painful to you."

"You know, it wasn't? That was always the strange thing about my friendship with Leila. We understood each other so well that the physical side of things, however pleasant, was not essential to us. It's hard to explain, but since you're so determined to know all, the act of love, or whatever you choose to call it, was simply another expression of our mutual understanding."

I was conscious of an odd mixture of emotions, but I'm afraid the primary one was jealousy. Here, through all the years, this seemingly docile son had been receiving such inspiration as he needed from another family source! It was bitter tea.

"You must miss her terribly" was all I could say.

"Oh, we write often. And she's planning a trip east, if Jim will allow it. She's made a clean breast of everything to him, and he evidently doesn't much care. Of course, he's had plenty of diversions of his own. But you needn't be concerned. Whatever we do, we will not renew the affair. Leila is most clear about that."

"And it was all over at the time I thought you were making up to Marjorie?" Oh, it was I who was in for it now!

He was indignant. "Mother, do you think I could flirt with a girl while I was having an affair with another? What sort of man do you think I am?"

"I guess I'm beginning to find out," I answered ruefully. "Would you say you were in love with Leila?"

"Love? What is it, really? There was always peace between us, never torment. Certainly Proust wouldn't have called it love."

"Were you in love with Marjorie?"

"Mother, you really are the limit tonight! What's eating you? No, I don't think I was in love with Marjorie, but I may have been on the verge, because Leila left a vacuum and Marjorie was an attractive person to fill it."

"What stopped you then?"

"You can ask that question?" he threw at me. "You, who told me she was a hopeless alcoholic? And that you'd practically expire if anything happened between her and me? I don't say I'd have given up the love of the ages to oblige you, but the little thing that existed between me and Marjorie was not too great a sacrifice to make for a desperate parent."

He took in, without in the least comprehending it, my sudden look of despair, and tried to console me, offering me another drink, but I pushed the poor bewildered man aside and took myself up to a sleepless bed.

The next day was Sunday, on which I always called on my mother-in-law. I hoped that this time it would provide a distraction from my misery, but, alas, it made things worse. Our discussion at once fell on Marjorie's death, and, or course, it was like Grinnell's nasty old mother to try to lay the blame of the tragedy at my door.

"A terrible thing, this, about the Gleason girl," she announced solemnly.

"Isn't it? But we can be grateful that nothing came of her friendship with Damon."

Mrs. Scott stared at me over her pince-nez. "But we all thought you had been pushing it!"

"Until I decided that her drinking was incurable. As we now only too clearly see it was."

"Do we? And if it was, I should have thought you had always known that. Wasn't it indeed one of her attractions?"

"How do you mean?"

"Well, wasn't it like that novel of Henry James's?"

I gaped. I reviewed in my mind some of the titles. "You mean *The Wings of the Dove*!" I exclaimed in horror. "You mean Damon would have married a dying heiress to inherit her money? Mrs. Scott, you can't believe anything so dreadful!"

"What would have been so wrong? The Gleason girl would have died happy, for everyone said she was crazy about him, and he would be rich, instead of still living, as he does, with you and Grinnell. I can't say you've done very well, my dear. You may have broken that poor girl's heart. And who knows? Married to Damon, she might have given up the bottle."

I left the house as soon as I could to go home on the path through the woods that separated our dwellings. Nor did I once look back. Like the ancient mariner, I dreaded to see the fiend that close behind me trod.

Collaboration

In my youth in the 1930s, my parents had a summer home by the ocean on the south shore of Long Island in Cedarhurst, only an hour by rail from the heart of the great city, where my father went daily to his stock exchange firm, except in his vacation month of August, which he devoted to golf. Our house, at the end of a dead-end street called Breezy Way, was a large white-shingle affair, called the Bray, because it had once boasted stables, and was separated from the sea by a wide marshland on which it was my delight to take lonely rambles. Far enough out in it, amid the numberless muddy inlets, the tall reed grass, the impenetrable sedge and the rushes, one felt a world away from the distant and barely visible cottages in a manless territory of seagulls, terns, sandpipers, frogs, muskrats and herons. It was here that I indulged in daydreams fraught with romantic fluff, unsullied by any of the stern practicalities of home.

I was not an only child but an only son; my sole sibling was my older sister, Edith, ever preoccupied with the social life of her contemporaries, who would never set a dainty foot on the muddy trail of the marshes. My father, rotund but athletic, hearty and well-meaning, but possessed of few interests beyond his stocks and his golf, was seemingly content in his marriage to my much more competent mother, a handsome, practical, socially minded woman, an excellent *mâitresse de maison*, who managed him as easily as she did the first families of the neighborhood who flocked to Breezy Way as to a natural leader.

I always felt that I was a distinct disappointment to both of my parents, as I was not good-looking, athletic or gregarious, and cared only for such passive activities as reading or listening to music or writing poetry. I must admit, however, that Mother rarely showed the chagrin that she surely felt, and wisely constrained my father into accepting her policy of allowing me freedom to indulge my tastes, so long as I conformed to the minimum standard she felt was needed to adapt me to the practical world in which I one day would have to live. I saw that, by her worldly rules, she was being fair, and did my best to obtain decent grades in the New England boarding school to which I, reluctant, was sent and which I cordially disliked. After all, I still had the long Cedarhurst summers.

The marshes were my other life; I may even say they were my real life. I learned to identify the most infrequently visiting warblers, and claimed to have sighted a prothonotary; I spotted the rare wood duck and once saw a bald eagle, our national bird, ignominiously chased by a smaller but fiercer osprey. Toward the middle of the summer most of our neighbors fled the heat for Maine or the Massachusetts shores, and there were no parties of young people that Mother could urge me to attend, so, taking a sandwich lunch and a volume of Keats or Shelley, I could pass the whole day alone. But one summer, when I was seventeen, another person appeared on the trails of the marshes, and this person, at first seen by me as an intruder, became my most valued friend. He was also, oddly enough, a stockbroker and a good friend of my parents.

I say "oddly enough," as it would not have occurred to me that a member of my parents' circle would have any use for the marshes or for me, and particularly such a one as Arthur Slocum, trim and elegant, still in his early forties, and married to a rich, vivacious and twice previously married woman, Leopoldine, commonly known as Polly, some years his senior, who shared with my mother the social rule of our little community. But Mr. Slocum, as I was to call him until my college days, differed from the family friends in that he shared my love of rustic solitude and won my trust at our first meeting on the brambled path that led from Breezy Way to my haunts by asking me, with an appealing deference to my greater experience, whether I would be his guide through the rough trails of the marshes. I was happy to show him all my little discoveries, and it soon became our habit to roam together by the creeks and rushes on weekend afternoons.

If tall and slender, he was also firmly built and smartly clad, even for a country hike, usually in soft gray, as if to match the thick and prematurely whitening hair that descended in a triangle over a high clear brow, pointing to the thin tip of his aquiline nose. His voice was low and grave, his articulation precise, and his blue-gray eyes twinkled with a mockery that was inconsistently gentle. He had been, I learned from my parents, a long-time bachelor, marrying late the woman he had adored and continued to adore, having awaited her through two messy divorces.

He was the first adult who had ever *listened* to me. My teachers at school were interested only in testing what I had learned, and my parents only in detecting some signs of a sensible maturity. But Mr. Slocum exhibited what I came to accept as a genuine desire to share with me the delights of poetry; he loved to quote and hear me quote bits of Shelley and Keats, and soon he was widening my literary horizon with choices of his own, particularly with samples of his idol, George Meredith.

"He's the only example we have, besides Hardy," he suggested, "of a man who was at once a great poet and a great novelist. In English, that is. The French, of course, have Hugo. Meredith shows us that no literary form is beyond the range of a great romantic."

That very night I found *Diana of the Crossways* in one of the standard sets in the family library and finished it by the weekend. Mr. Slocum then lent me his signed first edition of *Modern Love*, which I devoured, wondering whether the adultery of Meredith's first wife, which had so notoriously inspired the sonnet sequence, had a duplicate in Mr. Slocum's vision of his own wife's stormy love life. But I dared not ask him.

When, as our mutual trust developed, I confided in him some of my distaste for school and for Cedarhurst society, he reminded me forcefully of my blessings. "You have the marshes, Tony! You've had the sense to grab hold of them and make them your own. Never underestimate that, my boy. The terns and the gulls and the herons. And you and I may have the luck to spot again that prothonotary warbler you were lucky enough to sight."

"But what can I do with all that? When I'm a lawyer or a broker or whatever?"

"What does it matter what you'll *do* with it? You'll have your visions."

"Visions of what?"

He embraced our landscape with a wide gesture. "All of that. What you see today."

"You mean if I write it down? In a poem, say?"

"Well, yes, if you like, though it's not essential. I used to write sonnets in the trenches during the war about the old abbey in Normandy that my father converted into our summer house."

"Did you ever publish them?"

"Oh, no. They were no good."

"How do you know? Did anyone ever read them?"

"Never. They were just mine. A single poet and a single reader. It was a very satisfactory relationship. A very fine one."

"But isn't that selfish?" I asked, more boldly now. "Shouldn't beautiful things be shared? Suppose Shakespeare had burned *Hamlet* when he finished it?"

"Well, my efforts were not *Hamlet*. But I won't get into the pros and cons of publishing. What I suggest is that some great art may never have seen the light of day. Because it was utterly free of the egotism and passion for glory that consumes so many writers."

"You mean like Emily Dickinson locking up her poems?"

"Or Cézanne abandoning a canvas in the woods. Or Wordsworth leaving the *Prelude* unprinted for fifty years. I'm glad, of course, that those wonderful things were recovered for posterity; my only point is that the complete absence of ego, or its complete assimilation into the work created, may be a mark of great art. Like Emily Dickinson's slant of light on a winter afternoon. Do you know it?"

I asked him to recall it to me, and he recited slowly:

When it comes, the landscape listens—
Shadows—hold their breath—
When it goes, 'tis like the distance
On the look of death—

"Don't you feel that you're alone with the poetess, inside her brain, so to speak? I guess what I'm trying to tell you, Tony, is not to be afraid of your isolation. You're happiest here on the marshes. Oh, don't deny it; it can be a great strength and will do you for courage if we get into another war. Not that you don't have courage anyway—of course you do. But freedom from your fellow men can be a resource. It reconciles you to the great black void of the universe where the end of animate life, as Walter Pater put it, is like the setting of a pale arctic sun over the dead level of a barren and lonely sea."

I shuddered. "Is *that* such a comfort?"

"The comfort is in the beauty of the expression."

I sighed. "Well, maybe I'll come to see it."

I was always aware of what to me was the anomaly of so serious a thinker as Mr. Slocum being on such congenial terms with my parents and, indeed, with all of their tightly knit affluent and mundane little groups of Cedarhurst summer residents and year-round commuters. Of course, though he was their intellectual superior, his charm and modesty, to say nothing of his skill as a polo player, enabled him to amuse and divert them without arousing the least jealousy or resentment. Oh, yes, that explained their liking of him well enough, but why was he so content to shine unrivaled in a group that, however friendly and well meaning, was never challenging or even critical? Was he lazy? Or simply desirous of avoiding contradiction or dispute?

When I asked about this on our next meeting, he appeared to agree, if a bit ruefully, with my assessment of his choice of social life.

"Well, you see, it's Polly's world, my wife's world, or, you might say, *the* world, which Polly somehow epitomizes. You know, the jolly world, full of laughter and fun and good spirits, and success. Yes, success is part of it, part of the *real* world."

"And Mrs. Slocum represents all that?"

"Well, say she represents the best part of it. She helps keep me alive. Out here on the marshes, she says, I lose myself. I am no longer me. I'm dissolved. There's nothing left of the corporeal Arthur Slocum."

"Except his soul," I offered boldly.

What I wanted to get at was the unique value he placed on solitude. It was as if that was where his soul existed. Of course he was not alone when he was with me as we trudged through the marshes, but I took it that he regarded me as somehow indigenous to the territory, like a tern or a gull, and therefore not an intruder on his privacy. And certainly on our peregrinations he was a different man from the one I observed at a Sunday lunch given by my family. There was little enough in common between the brooding observer of flora and fauna and the quoter of romantic verse, and the genial tippler at Mother's long table who would always laugh the loudest at his wife's jokes, and the desperately serious polo player who was constantly taking spills in showing off his dubious prowess to a spouse more absorbed in the gossip of her box in the stadium. But which was the man he really wanted to be?

He responded now to my last remark about his soul.

"That is one way of putting it, I suppose. But if the soul is stripped down to its essence, isn't that a state of death? And I want to live, don't I? Doesn't every man? Polly to me is life!"

We trudged on in silence after this fervent exclamation, both a bit embarrassed by his outburst.

"It must be wonderful to feel that way about one's spouse," I said at last. "How did you and she meet?"

He was only too glad to reminisce. "It was five years ago at a polo match at Meadowbrook. Before the game I happened to walk by her box, and a mutual friend in it hailed me over. She was wearing a straw hat with an enormous brim, and as she turned to greet me, with a radiant smile that I supposed she gave any man lucky enough to be introduced, I was a goner. She was married at the time, Tony, but I knew I could wait for that woman forever if I had to! A man can get anything in the world if he really, really wants it. I believe that, my boy! I almost broke my neck that day playing polo. I wouldn't have given a damn so long as she noticed."

It was hard for me, at my age, to see his Leopoldine in quite the dazzling light in which he enshrined her. It was not that she was not interesting; she *was* interesting, even at times fascinating. She was hardly a beauty, but she may have been something of one when she was young; that is, younger than her present age of fifty. We knew she must be that old, for she had been in Mother's class in Miss Chapin's School. She was tall and thin and a bit boney, but her movements were graceful, and she was always elegantly attired with large, rather jangling jewelry. Her dark hair was drawn straight back over a noble pale brow; her features were large and handsome, and her big, roving, gray-blue eyes seemed, somehow intelligently, to be seeking something more amusing than what she was presently offered. At social gatherings, where I observed her, usually at my parents', she was animated and perhaps a bit grabby with the conversation, but she could be very funny, and when she wasn't, her loud, rather raucous laugh tried to make up for it.

Mother, who was inclined to be catty about her, said she drank too much.

It interested me to watch her with Arthur. I've said that her eyes were roving, but they always came back to him. She seemed intent on bringing him out, calling attention to his remarks and laughing loudly at his jokes, which she must have heard before, yet also correcting him, reproving him, almost at times shutting him up. It struck me that she treated him like a precocious favorite child who, from time to time, needed to be disciplined. And yet I must not overdo the maternal note, for it was obvious from the loving way she touched his arm, his hand, any available portion of him, that she was a doting spouse. Perhaps too doting.

Their relationship was the subject of much discussion in my family. Father's interpretation of it was crude but insightful: "Polly makes him feel like a man; she gives him balls. Arthur has always felt inferior to muscular types, like her first two husbands, who were both great college jocks. When she was finally free of the second, he jumped almost hysterically at his chance at achieving big muscles by becoming the mate of his antiquated Venus. Of course, she had what I call 'mileage'; she'd been all over the lot in addition to her two spouses, and even with her dough she was lucky to get anyone as respectable as Arthur for Number Three."

"I think you're right about her being desperate," Mother conceded. "But not about getting a third husband. You underestimate the lure of her fortune, which quite makes up for her age and other things. I suggest that what drew her to Arthur was that he fell head over heels in love with her at first sight and didn't give a damn about her age or money or previous affairs and marriages. He was like Alfredo in *Traviata*, bursting into rapturous song over an ailing prostitute, happy to throw away his future and career for her."

"I didn't call Polly a prostitute," Father objected. "If anyone had to pay, I'm sure it was she."

"Don't be so literal. What I mean is that Polly, middle-aged and battered, suddenly finds a glowing younger man who worships her for just what he sees in front of him—nothing else. I don't think anything like that had ever happened to her before. Don't forget that I've known her from way back. There's always been something essentially unlovable about Polly. Wherever you tap her, she rings a bit false. She's used her wealth to buy everything she thought she wanted in life, and what's she got? Nothing, or at least nothing that she now values. And suddenly here is love, steaming love, from what to her is almost a youth, handed her on a silver platter, something that at her age she can never expect to duplicate! Why of course she grabs it! And of course she's going to hang on to it, if she has to kill to do it. She'll eat him alive!"

I had an uncomfortable vision of the female insect that devours the smaller male after copulation. "But of course she can never be his intellectual equal," I muttered.

"Then she'll smother his intellect!" Mother exclaimed. "All I can say is, he'd better watch his step."

If Mrs. Slocum watched her husband as closely as Mother implied, then it was inevitable that she would take an interest in his marsh excursions even with someone as insignificant as myself, and indeed I got notice of this at a buffet Sunday lunch at my parents' when she chose me as her meal companion at a little table for two.

"My husband tells me, Tony, that you're an expert on the flora and fauna of our neighboring marshlands. Would you be kind enough to take me on a guided tour some afternoon?"

Well, of course, that was easily arranged, and the very next day at three she met me at the foot of our driveway on Breezy Way, smartly attired in red leather boots, tan slacks and a mauve sweater. She listened to me, as we walked, with polite but distant attention while I discoursed on birds and amphibians, and it wasn't until we had paused to rest, sitting on my favorite log, that I learned, without surprise, that she had other than Mother Nature's creatures in mind.

With a sweeping gesture she encompassed the marsh. "Tell me, my friend, just what my dear spouse sees in all this."

"Well, I guess you've got to feel it. If you don't, you don't."

"Meaning I'm hopeless?"

"Oh, no. Meaning you probably respond to other kinds of beauty."

"Thank you, Tony. You're a gentleman. It's true that I respond to art. To lovely paintings and drawings and sculpture and all the beautiful things that make up a handsome interior."

"So there you are. You're an interior person. Perhaps Arthur is an exterior one."

"An interior person." She sniffed. "It sounds like an odalisque."

I blushed, for that was exactly what I'd meant. "Oh, please, Mrs. Slocum..."

"Don't mind me," she interrupted. "I'm laughing at you. But seriously, don't you think that Arthur likes beautiful man-made things as well as natural things? His taste is not confined, is it, to crabs and muskrats and God knows what that teem in this—if you'll forgive me—somewhat smelly spot?"

"Oh, no!" I exclaimed in all earnestness. "He loves poetry more than anything. He loves all beautiful things, whether manmade or godmade. But he has this idea that there may be something vulgar in communicating one's sense of the beautiful. He likes to keep it to himself."

"Isn't that like a monk praying for his own salvation, locked away in a monastery?"

"I suppose you could say that."

"And doesn't he share it with *you?*"

Was it my morbid imagination, or did I detect something like jealousy in her tone?

"You know," she went on, in a more bantering way, "what some people may say about a middle-aged man who habitually disappears into the solitude of the marshes with a boy young enough to be his son?"

In my horror and disgust, I could only shake my head, and Mrs. Slocum uttered one of her loudest laughs. But what really appalled me was my curious impression that she might have actually preferred that her husband's relations with me should be sexual rather than intellectual. She could have coped with buggery!

"Well, you give me hope," she continued, in an almost businesslike tone. "If Arthur can share his love of beautiful things with you, perhaps he can share them with me. I'm sure that you agree he could do more with his life than sell stocks and bonds for a salary that we are far from needing."

"Oh yes! He should write."

"Well, maybe he'll come to that. But I have another plan, one to start with. He's just inherited that old abbey in Normandy where he grew up. His father gave his stepmother a life estate in it, and she recently died. Arthur supposes that we should sell it, but I have a better idea. Why not keep it, move over there, and fix it up with fine things? Make it into a *monument historique?* We could shop together, comb the Paris art galleries and *antiquaires* together and be partners in a work of art!"

"I think it's a wonderful idea!"

"It is, isn't it? Unless you happen to be wedded to Cedarhurst." She threw me a sly wink and rose to make her way back from a marsh that she would obviously never revisit. "And unless you can't live without crabs."

I thought her idea had merit and that Arthur might indeed find diversion in embellishing the old family abbey, but I was nonetheless uneasy. Remembering what Mother had said, I couldn't but speculate on the effect on him of the constant close attention of his daily and nightly partner in the enterprise, binding more and more tightly to him in the bonds of gratitude by what I was sure would be the reckless expenditure of her wealth.

On our last walk on the marshes before his move to France, Arthur was in a contemplative, almost melancholy mood.

"I'm going to miss all this, Tony."

"Even in beautiful Normandy?"

"Even there."

"But I'm told that when you and Mrs. Slocum are through with the abbey, it will burn on the water—of its moat, presumably—like Cleopatra's barge!"

"Oh, we'll do that, of course. And it will be amusing, I

suppose. The abbey will be fixed up, all right. As fixed up as possible. Within an inch of its life! When Polly decides to spend, get out of her way! But never forget, my boy, the marshes are just as good. The marshes may even be better. It comes pretty much to the same thing, though—the beauty of nature and the beauty of art. What is art doing but trying to excel nature?"

I didn't see the abbey until I graduated from Yale four years later and went abroad to spend the summer in Europe before starting at graduate school. It was the summer of 1939, and I had to scurry home when the war broke out, but I had time for a weekend visit to the Slocums'. The abbey was indeed gorgeous. The gray walls sloping over a richly kept lawn to a shimmering moat and formal French gardens; the long succession of lavishly appointed chambers, Venetian, Baroque, French eighteenth century, English Regency; the tapestries, bronzes, ceramics and paintings of every school, made it a choice museum that was open to the public three days a week.

Arthur was my grave and courteous guide who lost his gently mocking tone only when he spoke of the imminence of hostilities.

"I ended up in the last war hoping for peace at any price. I was like Siegfried Sassoon, only I didn't have his courage to speak out. But the irony of our situation is that *now* we are faced with the war that we thought the first one was: a crusade against the devil himself. The poor old Kaiser—*think* how warmly we'd welcome him as the German leader today!"

We ended our tour in the main parlor, and his wife caught his last remark.

"There may still be time for another Munich, Arthur!" she exclaimed.

"God forbid," he murmured.

But she heard him. "Do you want another war?" she cried, in a suddenly harsh tone. When he didn't answer, she turned to me, or perhaps I should say she turned *on* me. "As if one wasn't enough for him! One that cost Britain and France the flower of their youth and from which they've never recovered! Another war will finish them. Don't you agree with me, Tony?"

I stammered something about a man's not always having the choice, but she hardly heard me. If I wasn't an instant ally, I was an instant foe. She was older looking and more strident. The years had not improved her. She turned back to her principal target.

"So you don't care whether this house, with its priceless things, is blown to smithereens? Is that it, Arthur? Is that what it means to you, after all our work together?"

His tone was cautious. "I suppose there are things in life, my dear, that are more important than bric-à-brac."

"Bric-à-brac!"

"Well, art then, even the greatest art. Even Leonardo. Even the *View of Delft*, assuming we had it. Could you weigh it against liberty? Against freedom from a bloody despot?"

"Of course I could! Our job is not to fight for abstract ideas. It is to see that the beauty of the world is not destroyed. What is the liberty of one generation compared to the great monuments of art? Chartres has stood there for seven hundred years under despotism and democracies and is still there to inspire people with the reassurance of beauty!"

I supposed that the years Leopoldine had spent putting together a great collection had generated a certain passion for her creation—that was understandable, particularly in a woman of her capability and intelligence—but I couldn't rid myself of the notion that her animation was in fact caused by her husband's deviation from the tight union of spirits she had hoped to foster with her abbey plan.

"Darling," he said placatingly, "a war, if it comes, is not going to destroy all the châteaux in France. If, even at the worst, the Germans should overrun this part of the country, their army would probably take over the abbey for officers' quarters and treat it very well. And if America stays out of the war, they probably wouldn't occupy it at all."

I did not much admire this speech, but I could certainly see that the poor man was hard pressed. Leopoldine did appear somewhat mollified.

"Well, if you can promise me that," she said.

"Oh, my dear one, I can promise you nothing."

"But can you promise me you'll do everything in your power to save the abbey?"

"I can certainly promise you that," I'm afraid he said.

The war came, and devastated Europe, and in due course pulled America in. I did not have to experience my childhood nightmare of the trenches; I served more comfortably in the navy, where, if you were not sunk—and I had the good fortune not to be—you at least escaped mud and rats. I had no news from Arthur except that he and his wife had elected to remain in France even after the German occupation. When the Axis declared war on us, after the Japanese attack on Pearl Harbor, I had to assume that they had either been interned as enemy aliens or placed under house arrest in their beloved abbey. But on a leave to New York in the winter of 1943, I heard a different and distressing tale from Mother.

"I know how much you admired Arthur and how bad you will feel at what I have to tell you, but you're bound to hear it sooner or later, and you may as well get it from me. Henri de Villac, whose mother, you will remember, was an American and a great friend of my mother's, is over here, representing the Free French. He told me that the Slocums have been shockingly cozy with the German military from the very start of the occupation, entertaining high officers at the abbey and getting all kinds of dispensations. And that after we entered the war, a number of German officers were quartered at the abbey, not as conquerors but as welcome houseguests. The Slocums' new Boche pals saw to it that they got all the supplies they needed to make a jolly house party."

I felt too sick to make any comment, but at last I offered one. "I'm sure it was all *her* doing and just Arthur's weakness. She's a hard one to get around, once she's made her mind up. I suppose he couldn't bear to see her uncomfortable. To him she was always perfect."

"Oh, I don't in the least question her bitchiness. But you can't let Arthur off the hook quite that easily. You must remember that he always felt the first war had been a mistake. If we shouldn't have fought the Huns then, why fight them now? Let us at least save our bric-à-brac and pictures by kissing their asses!"

The war seemed to have brought out an unseemly coarseness in Mother, but what was I to say to it? I couldn't but remember what Arthur had told me about the folly of the first war.

I heard no more about the Slocums until the end of the war in Europe, which occurred while I was on temporary shore duty in London. A new British friend in my Grosvenor Square office, a liaison officer from their Intelligence, hearing me one day at lunch speak of my prewar visit to the abbey in Normandy, volunteered an interesting item.

"I'm afraid your friends were the worst kind of Nazi sympathizers. They got out of France, you know, right before the liberation of Paris. Just as well for them, too."

"No, I didn't know."

"With the help of some grateful German high-ups, no doubt. They went to Málaga."

"Where they still are?"

"Presumably. There are no charges against them. At least from us. Having been friendly to the Boches is not a crime so long as you didn't actively help them. But Mrs. Slocum had better stay out of France for a while. If she doesn't want to have her lovely head shaved. Or is it a wig?"

"No, it isn't."

"And there's another interesting side to the story. While they were wining and dining the Boches, their butler, one Gaston Robert, picked up some clues from the convivial chatter at the groaning board which he relayed to the Resistance and helped us to get a jump on the Jerries at the tussle at Bligny-sur-Oise."

I could have hugged him. For then I *knew*, but I thought it better to bide my time.

I was not able to go to Málaga until the end of the war in the Pacific. Discharged from the navy, I arranged for a short holiday in Spain before coming home, and I had no time to lose if I was to see Arthur, as word had reached me from Mother that he was dying of pancreatic cancer.

"It's probably as well," she wrote me, "because they could never again show their faces in France or America."

The villa in Málaga, on a hilltop with a fine view of the sea, large and white and airy, was evidence that Polly's dividends were still flowing in. She received me coolly, looking older and careworn, and asked no questions about my family or Cedarhurst.

"Arthur will be glad to see you," she said, in a noncommittal tone. "He spends his time in bed looking out the window. He hardly talks to me. We all have to meet our end in our own way, I suppose. He's not in much pain, fortunately. But that may come."

I found him pale and haggard, seeming resigned, almost indifferent to illness, to Spain and to me. On this first visit I chatted about my career in the navy, and he listened, politely but with little concern. When I left to go back to my hotel, I asked whether I could call again the next day, and he nodded.

But the following morning my attack was direct.

"I want to talk about your butler at the abbey, about Gaston Robert," I began bluntly. "I don't believe that he got the information that he fed to the Resistance merely by listening as he served at table. I believe he had help."

Arthur gazed at me in mild astonishment. "My dear boy, what on earth do you know about Gaston?"

"I know what British Intelligence knows. That he supplied the Resistance with some valuable tips picked up from German officers at the abbey."

"And you suppose that I assisted him?"

"I do."

"But, Tony, surely you know what people say about Leopoldine and me?"

I noted that he did not use her nickname, and I read a meaning into it. "Yes, but I don't believe a word of it. Certainly about you. That a veteran of the first war would have behaved that way is unthinkable. I remember what you used to say about keeping things to yourself. About the vulgarity of communication. Are you keeping your heroism to yourself? Please, Arthur, if you tell no one else, tell me! That's what I have come to Málaga for."

He was interested now. "If I'd been working with Gaston, why wouldn't the Resistance and British Intelligence have known it?"

"That's what I can't figure out. Did Gaston want all the glory for himself? I did discover that he was a rabid communist, and I speculated that he may not have wanted a bloated American capitalist to share in the birth of a new France. But then I wondered why you wouldn't have exposed his failing to give you any credit for his glory. If not for your sake, for your wife's."

Arthur nodded, slowly and thoughtfully. "Is this really that important to you, my friend?"

"Oh, yes!"

"And will you promise not to reveal what I say?"

"I promise. Unless you authorize me."

"Which I never shall. In the brief time that awaits me. Very well. I'll do it for you and for your ears alone. Because you do seem to care. And in memory of our marsh rambles." A small smile and a considerable pause followed before he resumed. "You were right about Gaston's communism. He didn't want his fellow Reds to know that he had an American goldbug as his partner. I believe he has ambitions of becoming a commissar in a Marxist Gaul and needs the glory of his wartime work for himself alone. And he's jealous, too. You were right about our partnership; I was very much the senior partner. Gaston would have had nothing without me; he wasn't very smart. But he had Resistance connections, which I needed, and he promised absolute secrecy as to his source, which was all-important to me, as my utility depended entirely on the Germans' trusting me. That was vital, and I knew that even the Resistance made slips. Sometimes fatal ones."

"But *now*, Arthur! Surely now it can be told!"

"Gaston has another hold on me, my friend. A shameful one, I fear. He has let me know, through his slave of a wife, who came to the abbey shortly before we left France, that if I claimed any share in his spying on the Boches, he would publish proof of the collaboration with them of a person close to me. A collaboration that might easily be classified as criminal by a France freed at last from the grip of her ancient enemy."

We did not have to name Leopoldine. I could only stare at the floor. When I looked up, Arthur's eyes were closed; he wanted to rest. Then the nurse came in, and I had to depart. I took no leave of my hostess.

I did not see Arthur again. I was told at the door the next morning that he had lost consciousness, and ten days later he was dead.

Arthur's wife returned to France, after the resentments of wartime had somewhat simmered down, and reoccupied the abbey. After she had given it and its treasures to France as a *monument historique*, reserving for herself only a life estate, her social position was much improved, although there was always a certain odor attached to her name. She continued to buy objects d'art for the abbey and became renowned for her sharp eye and expertise. The younger generation, often bored with the past, took delight in her wit and lavish parties.

I shall release this memoir when I hear of Leopoldine's demise, and I have given my instructions to my executor, should I die before her, as to how to make it known. Arthur's secret will not have gone to the grave with him.

I have often speculated as to why Leopoldine went as far as she did in her collaboration with the Germans. I have a dreadful suspicion that she may have discovered by chance, or guessed, that Arthur was communicating with the Resistance. Surely he would never have told her, partly for security reasons and partly to keep her out of it in case the Germans discovered him. But to her it may have been a repetition of his old severance from her ties, not unlike his walk on the marshes, and by dragging him down into the fetid embrace of a shared collaboration she would have joined him to herself forever. He would not share his heroic act with her, so she would make him share her shame. Perhaps not, but she was capable of it, and I will remember that at Málaga he never once referred to her as Polly.

The Justice Clerk

MY EXEMPTION from military service in the Second World War, on account of a limping and slightly shrunken left leg, the relict of a childhood bout with polio, has sorely intensified my lifelong sense of my greater exemption from all manly activities, and as I sit at my desk, as a tax lawyer in the Wall Street firm of Haight and Dorr, now deserted by a good half of its clerks and younger partners summoned to battle, I feel acutely the relative powerlessness of the written word, once my sole tool in the struggle of life.

I went into law originally, some eight years ago, because in college I had proved myself a third-rate poet and a worse spinner of short stories, and hoped to make a better use of words in briefs and arguments. I was an only child whose mother had died young in the flu epidemic of 1918 and whose grief-stricken father, a free-lance accountant with too few accounts, had somehow managed, in the teeth of the Great Depression, to put me through college and law school at New York University before he too expired. I hope it was of some consolation to the poor man, who gallantly tried to hide his obvious dismay at my poor physical condition, that my law school grades were the highest and that on graduation I was chosen as a clerk by a United States Supreme Court justice. For these goals I had toiled night and day and sacrificed such social life as might otherwise have come my way. Yet solitary as my academic life was, it still brought me Nora, my ex-wife, then an NYU undergraduate whom I had met as we were eating our sandwich lunches on the same bench in Washington Square.

I can see now what I should have seen from the beginning: that Nora, a small, pale, plain, raven-haired and intense young woman, was the type who would take people up violently and then put them down with equal violence when their opinions or acts have ceased to jive with her own. I should also have seen that there was little in my physical appearance to arouse her libido. Why, then, did she marry me? For it was she who proposed the match, not I, one day on that same bench. The answer is obvious enough. On her graduation, in the same spring as mine, no job, or even the distant prospect of one, awaited her. She faced a bleak future in Manhattan, living with an ailing mother almost as poor as herself, while through me she could visualize the excitement of Washington in the tumultuous days of the New Deal! It was an easy choice—for her.

And then, too, she had been intrigued by my position as an editor of the law review. She herself had wanted to study for the bar, but there were no further funds for her education. Her courses, all in modern history and economics, had brought her as close to the law as she could get. She was inclined to see it as a tool for the disadvantaged, as a substitute, perhaps, for riots or, indeed, for revolution.

On our dates she liked to discuss articles that she had read in my law journal and asked why I did not solicit more pieces on social unrest and injustice. As I had had little or no experience with girls, I was flattered by her interest in the only field where I had anything remotely like expertise and enjoyed answering her questions, sometimes at length, probably at too great length. I recall the following exchange, which shows the diverse directions in which we were heading.

"What made you first decide to become a lawyer?"

"Because it was a profession where I could use words. They were the only tools I had."

"But aren't they what everybody uses? What else is there? Muscle?"

"It's a matter of degree. I have only words."

"And what's so great about them? Aren't Hitler and Mussolini bewitching their countries with words?"

"Bad words. Which will be followed by guns. Bad words usually are."

"But so are good words. In Russia they were followed by a revolution that liberated millions from virtual serfdom."

"I think they were bad words. They led to the slaughter of the Imperial family in that cellar in Ekaterinburg."

"Surely, Peter Mullins, you can't defend the czar and his idiotic wife, who let a mad monk oppress their nation!"

"But why did the Reds have to gun down that poor little boy and the four innocent grand duchesses? Did you ever see those old films of them, all in white with big hats, so lovely and smiling, waving from a carriage at shouting crowds?"

Nora gazed at me in genuine perplexity. "You've got to be kidding," she said at last. But I wasn't. Then she went on, deciding, evidently, not to comment on so poor a joke. "What in your opinion is the difference between good and bad words?"

"Good words lead to sympathy and understanding, to peaceful settlements of controversies and general good will. Bad words lead to usurpations and seizures of power."

"What about the words of the Gospels? They led to the power of the Christian church."

"And to the Inquisition and the religious wars."

She looked at me with more approval now. "Didn't Marx say that religion was the opiate of the poor?"

"Well, there you are."

"And what about the words of the Constitution? Didn't they help to make America a great power?"

"No!" My exclamation was now triggered by sincere emotion. "They had nothing to do with power! Indeed, they were specifically designed to restrict power. They created our wonderful system of checks and balances. Which is currently in danger of being overthrown by the federal government's grabbing of powers inherent in the states."

"My economics professor says that the Constitution is nothing but an elastic band that can be stretched to encompass any old political philosophy that happens to be held by a majority of the Court."

"That's a very superficial view."

"You think it means what the Founding Fathers intended it to mean?"

"Well, to a much greater extent than most academics believe today. You couldn't assemble, at this point in our history, a constitutional convention with a tenth of the brains and vision of the 1787 one, even though our population has increased fiftyfold."

"So what they drafted, according to you, was like the tablets that Moses received on Mount Sinai?"

I don't think Nora was being as sarcastic as that sounds. She was still of the opinion that she had some things to learn from me, and she had not yet lost her awe of the law school.

"Something like that," I muttered.

"Yet those wise men tolerated slavery. It was written right into the original document, wasn't it?"

"An amendment wiped it out."

"Yet God, like Homer, must have nodded when it went in."

"If you like. It was a necessary compromise at the time. The price of our union."

"And the seed of a war."

"Alas."

"And wasn't it one of your good words that brought about that wicked compromise?"

"You have me there, Nora."

Justice Irving P. Davenport, of the U.S. Supreme Court, whose law clerk I was to be, had, though born a Virginian, practiced for many years in a large Wall Street firm, which was why he had adopted the habit of selecting his clerks from schools in the city. A partner in his old firm was delegated in each instance to make the choice for him, and it so happened that the one in my year was a devoted graduate of NYU who had himself been editor-in-chief of the review and regarded me in the light of a successor. When I informed Nora of my acceptance, on our now habitual bench, she flung her arms around my neck and announced that she would marry me! And as early as the following Labor Day we were established as man and wife in a two-room flat in the District of Columbia.

Judge Davenport was an impressive enough figure to meet. He was a tall, straight, handsome but rather stiff septuagenarian, with a long, lean, brown countenance and snowy white hair. His manners were formal and minimally courteous; he was patently a man not to suffer fools gladly nor to tolerate any intrusion on an attention usually devoted to matters weightier than the intrusion boded. He had been a lifelong bachelor without either of the customary excuses, so far as I could make out: a youthful unrequited affection or the tragic loss of a beloved. He seemed independent of all human support and lived rather opulently alone, except for two devoted and silently efficient black servants, a butler and a cook, in a beautiful red-brick Georgetown house, full of fine books, furniture and pictures. He had apparently made a fortune at the bar in New York.

He was known to be capable of singular rudeness where one of his prejudices was involved—I soon saw that he was barely civil to Justice Brandeis—but he was sufficiently agreeable to me, if on the gruff side, probably because of my bad leg and the fact that I was quick at my work and asked him a minimum of questions. Although I went to his house frequently in the evening when he wanted to work at home, he invited me and Nora only once to dinner, during which repast she, out of awe or timidity, hardly opened her mouth. The judge's social life seemed to consist of an occasional stag "breakfast," really an early lunch, to which he would invite a handful of elderly savants.

What I loved about him from the beginning was his fine use of the English language. His opinions were by far the most elegant of any written by the Court; sentences with the lapidary succinctness and arresting style of Emerson would be qualified by longer ones imbued with the grace and polish of Walter Pater.

"But isn't he to the right of Louis XIV?" Nora demanded one evening after reading one of his opinions that I had brought her. "If Madame de Maintenon complained, about Versailles and its gardens, that she perished in symmetry, isn't social progress going to perish in your boss's lavender prose?"

Well, of course, it was true that Nora's question was being irately put by half the editorials in the liberal journals of the day. A narrow majority of five judges (Davenport was one) was widely accused of engrafting onto the Constitution the economic doctrine of laissez-faire, which had not existed when the document was written. That very day at noon, when I was having a sandwich in my office, the judge, who had come in to get a book from my shelves that I had taken from his library, but whose step I had not heard, saw over my shoulder the newspaper that I was reading, open at the editorial page.

Snatching the paper from my hand, he snorted, "You're not paid to read that trash!" He tossed the journal back on my desk and proceeded to the door, but then, as if seized by a compunction, he paused and turned to me. "I'm sorry, Mullins. It's your lunch hour, isn't it? Of course, you can use it to read what you like. But maybe it's time that you and I had a little discussion about our personal views on the Constitution. Come to my office when you have some time."

Needless to say, I had time very shortly, and I found myself ensconced in the armchair facing his big flat unpapered desk while he held forth solemnly, as follows: "These parlor-pink whippersnappers on radical rags love to accuse me of being the compliant tool of the great corporations. Nothing could be further from the truth. I worked for many years as counsel to such corporations, yes. That's what a lawyer does;

he represents clients. And I chose to represent clients who could pay for my services. And pay well, to be sure. Is there anything wrong with that? The laborer is worthy of his hire. My firm did its share—more than its share, for that matter—of pro bono cases. Although I didn't work on these myself, what I brought in paid the salaries of those who did. But to deduce from all this that I was in any way governed by, or that I admired, the men in charge of those corporations is grossly unjust. My job was to keep their proceedings within the law, and I did. Nor was it always easy. I worked at times with individuals who, left to themselves, might have made mincemeat of legislative prohibitions. But they knew that if they did so, Irving Davenport would promptly withdraw as their counsel, and the world would make its own deduction as to why he had done so. And your radicals say that I admired such men? I most certainly did not! I agreed totally with Charles Francis Adams, Jr., when he wrote in his memoirs that he had worked with many of the greatest business tycoons of his day and had found them a dull and uncultivated lot. I never had any social dealings with such men; I saw them only in my office or theirs. Pierpont Morgan was the only gentleman among them, and he felt pretty much as I did. At least he knew a good etching or oil painting when he saw one. Or a good bronze." He pointed to a David holding up the head of Goliath on a table in the corner. "I got that one at the executors' sale of some of his art in 1914."

I realized that I was expected to fill in the pause that followed. "I suppose we can't expect the average journalist to distinguish between representing a client and admiring him."

"It's too much, no doubt, for his pea brain. And he carries his delusion to the limit. The judge who finds something unconstitutional must think it's bad, and if he finds it constitutional he must think it's good. That's their simple idea of how we interpret the Constitution."

"Would it be in order, sir, to ask what you think of the doctrine of laissez-faire and to what extent, if any, it should be abrogated?"

"It's more a question, isn't it, of who should abrogate it? The Constitution gives the federal government certain specified powers; everything else is left to the states. But today Uncle Sam is grabbing the whole kit and caboodle. What the New Dealers are doing is changing the original concept of a union of semi-independent states to that of a single nation, with the result that our vital rights and liberties will be protected not by forty-eight state governments and one federal one, but by one federal one alone!"

"Yet the Democrats talk a great deal about civil rights."

"And talk is all it is. To convince the unwary that the right of free speech, which Justice Holmes aptly called 'the right of a fool to drool,' makes up for all the other rights that are being filched from him: the right to manage his own business, to hire or fire whom he pleases, to produce what he wants in such quantities as he desires; in short, the right not to have the commerce clause flung in his face every time he happens to spit across a state line!"

We talked, or rather the judge talked, for another hour, and when I returned to my office it was with a new and exhilarating idea of the battle that he and I were engaged in. For wasn't such a struggle the very thing of which I had dreamed as the ultimate test of the use of words as the redemption of mankind? The fervent advocates of the New Deal may have convinced themselves that only a vastly increased federal force could save the nation from its economic depression, and that such was a humane enterprise, but that was because they were blind to the naked power drive behind it. The judge and I were fighting with the golden words of the Constitution to preserve an America as conceived by its Founding Fathers.

The next year and a half was the most intense and exciting period of my life. The attention of the nation turned more and more to the Court, and a growing chorus of voices in the halls of Congress, in the editorial pages of the press and at political gatherings from coast to coast were loudly and angrily raised to denounce the five judges who were steadily invalidating much of the New Deal's principal legislation. "Must we remain mired in a near feudal past because of the outdated philosophy of five stubborn old men?" was the gist of the cries that beset us from all sides.

But my chief was ebullient. He seemed to welcome the abuse. To him, he and his four judicial brethren were engaged in a heroic resistance to the rising tide of federal mega-government. What did it matter if they were slaughtered in the narrow pass of a twentieth-century Thermopylae? History would one day justify them. He led the way enthusiastically in seeking to strike down the excessive delegation by Congress of its powers to executive agencies, the prohibition of the shipment in interstate commerce of goods produced in excess of federal quotas, the establishment of pensions for railroad employees, the conferring of tax subsidies on "disadvantaged" groups, the providing of unemployment compensation and the fixing of minimum wages.

I was sometimes taken aback by how far my chief went, but I never ceased to admire his courage and force and, above all, the ringing clarity of the language of his opinions. His evocation of the fighting spirit of an America that had defied the monarchs of old Europe and conquered the western wilderness thrilled me, sometimes in spite of myself, and I could hardly help being impressed by the biting sarcasm with which he contrasted such a spirit with the red tape and muddled bureaucracy of the present. Unlike some of the other law clerks, I never wrote a word of his splendidly composed opinions, but I supplied the authorities and discussed with him the presentation of his arguments. He was sufficiently pleased with my work to extend my clerkship first with a second year and then with a third. I wasn't sure it was the best thing for my law career to remain in this position so long, but I couldn't bring myself to leave him in the midst of such a battle. And besides, wasn't it the battle of words?

I worked long hours, sometimes as many as four or five nights a week. It didn't hurt my marriage, because that was going too badly to be further hurt. Nora had taken a scantily paid job as the Washington reporter of a small radical New York magazine, and she followed congressional debates and committee hearings with an interest that swelled along with her own leftist leanings. She had lost all of her old awe of my superiority in legal matters and had nothing but freely voiced contempt for my enthusiasm for Justice Davenport. And she was too doctrinaire not to follow up her contempt for an opinion with contempt for its holder.

"What do you think of the President's Court bill?" she demanded sharply one morning, as we were drinking coffee before our departure for work. Her pale face loomed at me accusingly across the table.

"I think it's an outrage, of course. He wants to stack the

Court with new appointees whom he can trust to tear up the Constitution. There's been nothing like it since the Rebs fired on Fort Sumter."

"Only it may prove more successful."

"It'll never pass."

"Don't be too sure. I have a closer eye on the Hill than you do. And anyway, whether or not it passes, it may scare those old birds out of their hatchet work."

"My old bird doesn't scare easily."

"I'll bet that's so. But remember, we need only one of that unamiable quintet to change what he may wrongly call his thoughts."

"We?"

"Yes, my dear Peter, we. In case you haven't observed, I've moved considerably to the left, and I now regard the whole New Deal as basically much too conservative. Also, my paper wants me to move back to New York to take over a weekly column."

"And you're going?"

"Damn right, I'm going. It's a big promotion."

"Does this mean that you're leaving me?"

"It means I'm leaving Washington."

It was odd how little it took to sunder our marriage. I supposed that was because so little had gone into putting it together. When Nora was through with a man, she tossed him away like a used Kleenex.

The judge and I had become almost intimate as we worked together over his opinions. He associated little with his brethren on the Court, even with those of his persuasion, and his truculent reputation kept the other clerks from dropping in to our offices. When he inquired politely once about my wife's health and general welfare, and was told that she had moved to New York, he asked no further questions, but a few days later he invited me to save my rent money and move into a spare bedroom in his big house.

"You'll have regular meals, and good ones, and if we should work at night in my library, you won't have that long walk home. And my good butler will give you all the drinks you want."

I was delighted, as the judge already comprised most of my social life in the capital, and I figured that if, as I planned, I should one day write his biography, our new proximity would give me ample opportunity to glean information about his earlier decades. But I had not been long ensconced in my comfortable new quarters, and made welcome by the two servants, who were glad to have a younger presence in that staid atmosphere, than I discovered a side of my host that was not agreeable to see.

It may indeed have been a new side of his nature, brought out by the striking events of that time, rather than a festering sore that had suddenly erupted. We had witnessed the defeat of Mr. Roosevelt's Court-packing bill and had prematurely rejoiced, only to discover that the victory was decidedly a Pyrrhic one. For under the agile maneuvering of the chief justice, one of our majority of five defected, and the era of invalidation of grasping legislation was over. With the resignations that followed, the President at last had the Court that his defeated bill would have given him, and the New Deal was the law of the land.

My chief took it badly, too badly. He lost his biting humor

and became overtly vindictive. At our dinners together he signaled constantly at his disapproving butler to refill his wine glass, and in the library afterward, even when we were working, he had a whiskey and soda before him.

"It's all over now," he would mutter, half to himself. "That happy-go-lucky Hudson River squire can do anything he wants with our sacred rights and privileges. There's not much to choose between him and the man Hitler, except that Roosevelt won't go after the Jews. Isn't he one himself? Don't they say his name was changed from Rosenfeld?"

More prejudices, alas, than anti-Semitism began to emerge from his objurgations. I noted in him, to my considerable dismay, a tendency to slander opponents, actual or potential, to his way of thinking, with the peculiar meanness of certain extreme right-wingers. I offered no objection, for such was not my function, and anyway I knew it would be futile. If, for example, our discussion fell on questions of unemployment insurance, he was apt to comment on the laziness or unwillingness to work of many of its recipients and would quote such canards as the old one of the man who came to pick up his paycheck in a chauffeur-driven Cadillac. He would carry this over into the field of criminal law, suggesting that the victim in a rape case may have invited the attack by her scanty attire or loose conduct, and opining that the execution of an innocent person through a misidentification was not so grave a matter if the man was believed to have committed other heinous crimes.

I suffered under this for several months, but my breaking point did not come until the day when I was walking home with the judge after a day's work, and a reporter tagged along beside us, popping impertinent questions at the grimly stalking and unresponsive figure of the jurist. At last, about to concede defeat, he flung a final query.

"Are you ever going to retire, Mr. Justice?"

At this, the judge, having to pause for a red light, swung his head around at the young man and snarled, "Not while that son-of-a-bitch of a cripple is still in the White House!"

The reporter gasped and fled, and I was silent all the way to the house. But I had made up my mind, then and there, to resign my clerkship, and on the following Monday I informed my chief that I had decided the time had come for me to get started in the active practice of law. He could hardly object, as he had felt it incumbent on him to warn me not to overdo my time as a law clerk, and he was good enough to give me a glowing recommendation to his old Wall Street firm, where I am an associate to this day.

When I returned to New York, I had a meeting with Nora to see whether there was anything left of our marriage. She was very definite that there was not, and we agreed on an amicable divorce. She was already enamored of the editor-in-chief of her Red rag and had, I believe, become a card-carrying communist. We argued for a whole evening about the scandal of the Russian political trials, but she was adamant in her undying support of Stalin.

And so, disgusted alike with left and right, and the dangerous words that both employ, I have settled down to the euphoria of figures and try to lose myself in the blessed impersonality of taxes. Like death, they will always be with us.

He Knew He Was Right

New year's day is the morn for resolutions, and today, being the first of 1951 and opening a half-century, seems well timed. I take pen in hand therefore to record with an accuracy as scrupulous as my power permits, for the ultimate benefit of my two sons, now nine and ten, who are being raised largely outside my parental control, that they may understand, when mature enough to read this memorandum (which I shall leave with my lawyer to ensure its preservation) that their father was not the moral monster that their mother and her kin have depicted. Whatever the boys may conclude, they will have had the chance to hear my side of the story—the story, as I may put it, of my sexual philosophy and its application to my life.

My family background will be familiar to them; it is pretty much the same as their mother's. The Belknaps were old Manhattan of English source, Episcopal burghers of brownstone respectability, with the virtues and vices of their class. One of my father's grandfathers bought a substitute to fight for him in the Civil War; the other died in action, a gallant cavalry colonel. Few of the family stood out from the crowd, nor do I think they much wanted to. Pierce Belknap, my father, was a middle partner in a middle-sized but distinguished Wall Street law firm that bore the name of a deceased forebear to whom he largely owed his position. Stella, my mother, was known for her looks and charm, as well as for her almost too exquisite little dinner parties. We lived in a constantly redecorated brownstone on lower Park Avenue and spent our summers on the north shore of Long Island. I was sent, after years at the Browning School, to Saint Jude's, a church boarding academy for boys in New Hampshire, a great gray Gothic conglomerate where God may have once been and left. I had one sibling, a younger sister, Rhoda, who was shrilly and ineffectively at war with her family and life.

I was christened Robert, but Mother dubbed me Robin, perhaps in the disappointed hope that I would turn out gentler than I promised, and the name, which I have never liked, has stuck. I was hardly an amiable child, and certainly not like the bird that was my namesake, the herald of spring. If I was always strong for my age, I was sullen of disposition, dark-haired and dark-complexioned, an ugly enough brute, though my appearance improved as I grew up, at least in the eyes of one of the sexes. I may quote what my best (and sometimes, I think, my only real) friend, Newton Chandler, said of me once, perhaps not entirely jokingly: "Robin looked like a surly dead-end kid, but he was so quiet and stand-offish that one began to suspect he was hiding some inner sensibility, perhaps even a yearning for sympathy and affection, but when one approached him with this in mind, it was to find that one's first impression had been the right one."

Why was I thus truculent? I can't be sure, but I speculate that it had to do with some childhood concept of my parents being engaged in a losing battle that I could always see was bound to be lost. A battle against whom or what? Were they

Romans resisting barbarians? I don't know. Perhaps it was a battle against the whole world. And why was I so sure that it would be lost? Because I sensed the power of the barbarian in myself? Something like that.

Daddy was already lost; Mother was the real fighter, and I admired her just as strongly as I refused to show it. She was a distinctly pretty, slightly diminutive woman, with lovely large inquisitive greenish eyes, always perfectly clad for every occasion, without a spot on the white ensembles that she affected or a single one of her beautiful, genuinely blond hairs out of place. People were always saying that one had to be particularly trim and well-ordered when one went to Mother's house, but that, of course, was nonsense. Women like Mother don't give a damn what *you* wear; their rules apply only to themselves. And Mother carried this principle to an extreme. For some arcane reason—and she was not in the least religiously inclined—she apparently conceived of herself as the instrument of forces that required her interiors to be perfectly decorated, her entertainments exquisite, her guests provided with every amenity, and in her own life, her manners to be charming and her good deeds good. Now what, I would sometimes ask myself, in my rare efforts to be reasonable, was so wrong with all that, except for the toll that the constant industry took on her far from robust constitution? Wasn't that *her* look-out?

It might have been, had the toll not also fallen on Daddy. If the rest of the world had been exempted from the dark destiny that demanded such high standards of Stella Belknap, her husband had not been. His pledge at the altar had joined him ineluctably to her fate. I sometimes fancied that Mother must have chosen him with the same instinct that a parasite plant or animal chooses its host. Yet the relationship didn't seem to be one of symbiosis. I couldn't see that Daddy benefited from it in any way except for the obvious fact that he always adored her. Utterly compliant to her every demand, he never criticized her except for an occasional sly joke, half-whispered to a bystander and designed perhaps to convince the latter that he was more independent than might appear. If Mother overheard any such mild protest, she ignored it. She could readily distinguish between the muttered growl of an incipient coup d'état and the subdued squeal that may be safely—indeed, wisely—allowed the victim whom the gods had assigned to her task force to carry out, not her purpose, but theirs.

Daddy's professional life was spent in the shadow of his grandfather. Judge Belknap had been something of a figure in corporate reorganizations before his elevation to the bench, and my unhappy progenitor continually tried to convince his skeptical partners that his bearing the name of the deceased justified his share of the firm profits, which every year received a new slashing. For Daddy looked the part of a senior partner much more than he was one: tall, handsome, elegantly dressed, with fine graying hair and a commanding nose and chin. His full-length portrait in the reception hall provided an appropriate introduction to the long corridors of legal aptitudes, but it certainly did not reflect the strained inner tension of a man whose daily concern was preserving a diminishing income and an eroding capital to meet Mother's incessant demands.

It was not that Mother was unaware of financial problems. She would have been a perfectly good sport had they gone bankrupt and would have toiled as a cleaning woman to support him. Her dusky gods, as I dimly made out, would have asked less of her had the money been gone—it might even have come as a relief. It was simply her bounden duty—and, with marriage, now his—while the money was extant, to spend it as the powers demanded.

The curse, or whatever it was, was not extended to the children. Rhoda, who reacted with the contemptuous fury of a rebellious teenager to what she deemed Mother's worldly and snobbish standards, beat her head in vain against the wall of Mother's utter indifference to her protests. Mother would mildly deplore Rhoda's rudeness, her poor school record, her messy clothes and slangy remarks, but she accepted her as a convinced missionary might accept a Hottentot who was beyond conversion. Rhoda undoubtedly felt there was a lack of basic love in such an attitude, and I'm afraid Rhoda was right.

With me it was different. Mother loved me, and I, a bit reluctantly perhaps, loved her back. I sometimes wonder whether I am the only person she ever has loved. Father she owned, which was a different thing. But at the same time I think she was a trifle afraid of me, as if I represented, in some mysterious way, the very forces she was fated to fight and by which she was doomed ultimately to be overcome. Because for her gods, as well as Valhalla's, there had to be a Götterdämmerung. Perhaps one that she welcomed. Mother rarely criticized my carelessness in dress or manner, as she sometimes did Rhoda's. She acted as if I were something of a rule to myself. And when we talked, we could be curiously intimate. It was as if we were two generals of opposing armies, meeting alone in a tent between the lines during a truce and finding temporary relief in the brief shedding of our respective obsessions. I could forget I was a man, and she could remember she was a woman.

Daddy and I got on well enough, but basically I pitied his weakness. I suspect there were times when he wanted to talk more intimately with me—I thought I could read this in his soft, sad gray eyes—times when he may have wished to confide in me his worries about his law firm and Mother's expenditures, but then he must have checked himself lest it seem a disloyalty to his wife. When he visited me at Saint Jude's, he showed a particular interest in my prowess in football and never criticized me for my lack of sociability in taking so small a part in school extracurricular activities, as if he saw in my muscular development and preference for solitude an independence that I would be able to protect as he had not protected his own.

At Saint Jude's I was not exactly unpopular—my enthusiasm for the roughest kind of football and my skill at the game ensured me a certain respect—but I was not popular. My indifference to the values held dear by most of the boys would have subjected me to severe physical punishment had my ready, too ready fists not kept my schoolmates at bay, and my interference in the hazing of younger and weaker boys was considered a heresy to a sacred tradition. I didn't even have the satisfaction of imagining that I was a kind of Round Table knight coming to the rescue of the beset, for the surging fury I felt in my throat and chest when I beheld a boy attacked by others led me to a violence that on one occasion resulted in my near expulsion from the school. The headmaster himself informed me sternly that my reaction had been disproportionate to the cause and counseled me to consider in the future whether my urge to inflict punishment wasn't the same as what I sought to punish. Reluctantly, I conceded to myself that he might have a point, and made efforts thereafter to avert my eyes from scenes of threatened injustice. But this only intensified my innate insociability.

St. Jude's, like other New England church schools in the 1930s, was for boys and had only male masters. The faculty wives lived off campus and appeared only at occasional lunches in the dining hall and for Sunday chapel, and most of them had little enough appeal to a boy's wandering eye. And as for the cleaning women and waitresses, they had been picked by a housekeeper with an eye ready to spot and reject the least pretense of pulchritude. Movies were rarely allowed; home leave was granted only for family weddings or funerals; and it was rumored that saltpeter was put in our soup to reduce bestial cravings. The boys had recourse only to masturbation, solitary or what was called "mutual."

Though I was not popular, my muscular figure attracted its share of lewd invitations, which at first I scornfully rejected. But, hot with sexual frustration, I at last succumbed, though I was disgusted with myself for so doing and would hardly speak to my partner thereafter. I thought it a poor and degrading thing to do with one's sexual apparatus, and I would never have done it, for example, with my one friend, Newton Chandler, a small serious Boston boy whose high ideals seemed to me sincere enough not to be sneered at, and who had penetrated my reserve to discuss everything from our respective families to the existence of God, with a disregard for my churlish manners that I appreciate to this day. I knew that Newt disapproved of mutual masturbation, though he never mentioned it.

It was through Newt that I became a protégé of Mr. Trumbull, a young, naïve and passionately enthusiastic English teacher who took very seriously indeed his self-imposed mission to enrich the lives of schoolboys with romantic poetry. I am sure it was Newt who persuaded Trumbull, who came to the school on his first academic assignment in our last year there, that I might be an interesting convert, and the young master's friendship made those final months at Saint Jude's less lonely for me when Newt, because of a lung problem, had to spend the winter in New Mexico.

My classmates and I were seventeen, and senior year gave us more privileges. I could spend a Sunday afternoon at the Trumbulls' house if I was invited or take a canoe alone on the river. We had graduated from nighttime sexual games in the dormitory; we met girls at dances on vacations, and some of us engaged in amorous correspondence. I enjoyed reading poetry and discussing it with Mr. Trumbull. His pretty but sullen young wife sometimes sat with us and listened, but after a while, undoubtedly bored, she would take herself off. She would look at me, however, and I was old enough to know what her look meant. I hardly dared to think that she meant anything more, but I thought of her lustfully at night.

Wordsworth was Mr. Trumbull's favorite poet, and I recall a heated discussion that he and I had about the sage of Grasmere's proposition that "one impulse from a vernal wood" could teach us more of man than all the philosophers of yore. I maintained that Wordsworth had lived before the age of magnified camera studies of insect and plant life, which showed the never-ending consumption of one species by another.

"Why, even the plants do it!" I exclaimed. "There are those which close their petals to catch some poor feeding bug. It's eat or be eaten. That's your impulse from that vernal wood. Nature is savage. And man is savage!"

"Even civilized man?"

"Who's civilized? The great so-called civilizations have been the result of bloody conquests. There's a savage in every soldier."

"You admit no exceptions?"

"Well, maybe the Romans. A little. In Rome they disciplined the savage in themselves to create a force that could bring order to a world of warring nations."

"You'd like to have lived in Rome, Robin?"

"I wouldn't have minded."

"And killed people?"

"Haven't you ever wanted to kill anyone, Mr. Trumbull?"

I remember how he shuddered. "Not consciously." And then it was like him to go off on a tangent like the following: "But those horrible games in the arena; would you have liked going to *them?*"

"Oh, that was later, in the Empire. They probably picked up bad habits from the Carthaginians. No, the Republic would have been my affair. When you could put the brute in you to work—useful work. Killing raiding barbarians. Quelling silly religious wars. Policing the world."

"Religion? Would you have liked a religion where gods seduced mortals and turned them into trees and things?"

"No sillier than one whose god created sinful men in order to redeem a chosen few."

"You're not even a monotheist?"

"No. I'm not sure I believe in any god. But if I have to believe in one, why shouldn't I believe in many? Why is believing in one considered such an advance over paganism? The headmaster in sacred studies is always prating about how the Jews had a genius for religion because they invented Jehovah. But I prefer Olympus! I want Venus *and* Mars, and I like to think of them caught bareassed in the act by Vulcan's net!"

I was still immature enough to want to shock my one faculty friend, and his wife, of course, was out of the room when I made my last remark. But I had reason later to believe that she was standing just outside the door. As I have said, she was pretty, a lively brunette with a trim figure, and it was certainly not to hear my silly historical theories that she eavesdropped. Why had she married Trumbull? Probably to get away from something worse. I knew nothing of her background except that it was obviously a humbler one than those of the other school wives. She must have had a mean enough social life on campus.

Mr. Trumbull's next comment on my religious speculations showed that he was at last alarmed at how far he may have permitted me to travel mentally beyond the school compound. "I hope you don't say these things, Robin, to anyone but me. People, even schoolmasters, don't much care what you think. But what you say—I mean what you say seriously—is another matter."

But I was approaching a crisis in my life that involved neither thinking nor saying, and was more important than either. And once again it was poor Mr. Trumbull who indirectly—most indirectly—supplied the occasion.

One Sunday afternoon, as I was making my solitary way to the river, a woman stepped into the path from the woods some distance ahead of me. As she was evidently awaiting me, I accelerated my pace and discovered it was Mrs. Trumbull.

"May I join you, Robin?"

I knew at once that something was up, but my throat was so thick and tight that I could only nod.

"There's a nice little path down to Merrill's Pond," she continued in a flat tone. "No one ever seems to use it. We can have it all to ourselves. Just Venus and Mars. No Vulcan."

Again, I nodded and followed her lead. I could hardly breathe, in my excitement and anticipation. Then, suddenly, but as if in accordance with a plan, she struck into the forest and we made our slow way through underbrush to a little clearing, where she took off her coat and spread it on the ground. When she spoke, her tone was clear and definite.

"Remember. What we need never admit never happened."

After which she quickly stripped, and I followed suit, again without a word. I had a moment to reflect that she showed an ease and habit that must have been learned before her match to poor Trumbull. She helped me and guided me, but I didn't need much teaching, and on our third orgasm I felt I had graduated from a tyro to Don Juan. When I think of all the literature that has been written about the awkwardness of initial sexual encounters, it seems a miracle that the pleasure of my first adventure has been equaled but never surpassed.

Mrs. Trumbull and I found occasion to repeat our experience twice before my graduation in June, after which she and her husband went west, to a school where he had been offered a better position, and I never saw them again.

Yet the affair, if it merited the term, changed my life. I was exhilarated, inebriated; in short, I was a new man. All guilt about sexual fantasies and sexual acts vanished away; I might have been Siegfried, who had braved Loge's fire to mount

Brünhilde. I was sure that I had done the right thing, physically, spiritually, even morally. Mrs. Trumbull had needed me, needed me badly. I hadn't taken anything from her husband that he really wanted, and his wife was probably half-crazed by his obsession with Wordsworth and his smug assurance that an occasional hug and some hasty Saturday night coitus would satisfy her. What he didn't know would never hurt him and might even save his marriage.

Except that it didn't. Some two years later, when I was a junior at Yale, I heard that the Trumbulls had broken up. Mother told me, on a weekend when I was home, after the guests at one of her Sunday lunches had departed and she and I were sitting alone together, over a half-finished crême-de menthe, in her lovely living room.

"Agnes Seely told me. She has a boy there, and it appears there was some sort of scandal about an affair with another master. I pricked up my ears because Trumbull was the teacher —was he not?—with whom you were so close your last year at Saint Jude's?"

"Not really," I replied. "We never saw eye to eye. Still, it was nice to have someone in that stuffy academy to talk to. But it was his wife who really taught me about life."

"I hope you don't mean what you seem to mean."

"Oh, but I do." Mother had now become my nearest confidant, closer than Newt, with whom I roomed at Yale. I liked to watch the avidity with which her curiosity and fascination overcame her prudish inheritance. She must have felt that the best way to help her beloved firstborn was to understand him, and I think that she was quite right. As I believed that *I* was quite right in helping her widen her moral horizon and live in what I conceived to be the real world. So I told her about myself and Mrs. Trumbull.

"Adultery, Robin! At barely eighteen! Did you have no feeling that what you were doing was wrong?"

"None at all. We didn't *tell* Trumbull; we took great care not to tell a soul. Any wrong would have been in the telling. The doing was what nature called on us to do. And we were both the better for it."

"Are you telling me, Robin Belknap, that there's nothing wrong with men and women making love—if *that's* what you call it—whenever they choose, regardless of their commitments to others?"

"I'd qualify your 'whenever.' As a matter of taste, I shun promiscuity. And I think the greatest care should be taken to avoid unwanted pregnancies or to cause jealousy in those with more restricted views."

"More restricted views! I like that! I suppose you mean some benighted old-fashioned husband or wife."

"Exactly. To me it's all a matter of tact and not of morals. If two people can satisfy their deepest and most natural urges without outraging others, I see no wrong in it."

"But how can they? Look at your Trumbulls. Do you think she never threw in her husband's face what a better time she probably had with you?"

"I hope it was more than probably. But if she did, she did wrong. That's not my business."

"How can you say that, when you aroused her and excited her and very likely made her discontented with her marriage?"

"She was already that. But you may be right. Maybe I should take some blame for what happened to her marriage, though I think that was coming anyway. And remember that I was young and it was my first time and that she seduced me. I hope, if I get involved in another such situation, that I'll handle it better."

"But, my dear boy, these things, as you know, are very explosive. It's impossible to keep them secret."

"Difficult, certainly. Not impossible. But that's not the point. The point I'm making is that *if* one can keep them secret, they're no more immoral than an act of masturbation."

"Please, dear! I'm not as liberated as you."

"No, but you're getting there. Look, Ma. You know there's some sense in what I'm saying. You know I'm not an immoral person."

"Yes, I do know that. And you never have been. I remember as a boy how you blew your poor sister up when she kept library books out overtime."

"She kept dozens! And for months, too. I tried to impress on her that we weren't that kind of people."

"Everything's wrong but free sex? Is that it?"

"Well, isn't most people's moral code that everything's right but free sex?"

"Right?"

"In the sense of all right. Or not so bad. I leave out felonies. I'm talking about the moral code of the people we know. They put up with much more than I'm willing to: lying, cheating, exploiting, getting ahead of each other any way they can, pushing, shoving, showing a minimum of compassion or generosity. But when it comes to sex, whoa!"

"What would your father say to all this?"

"I wouldn't be having this talk with Dad. He's been broken by the system."

"You mean by me!"

"By you operating within the system. You're a victim, too, Ma. Only you know it. That's your salvation."

"Or my damnation. However, watch out, my child. What you believe could land you in serious trouble. And I won't have that, because I love you." She glanced at her watch. "And now you'd better go if you're going to catch the four o'clock to New Haven."

I sometimes fancy that society used Olivia, as the Philistines used Delilah with Samson, to betray me to my enemies. She was a Philadelphia girl, from Chestnut Hill really, of one of the oldest families, the Peytons, and she concealed, beneath her large but superbly shaped torso and her large handsome Grecian features, a conservatism that was all the fiercer for its studied suppression. A radiantly smiling Olivia gave the convincing appearance of being wide open to a new world and a world of new things. I met her at the Yale prom in my senior year, when she was Newt Chandler's date. Newt, with his usual excessive generosity, made no objection when I hardly left their side during the entire weekend. I was enchanted with Olivia from the beginning.

Newt and I had one of our frankest talks when the weekend was over and Olivia had returned to Chestnut Hill.

"No need to apologize for being such a buttinsky," he assured me coolly. "I am quite inured to your grabbiness. As a matter of fact, I invited Olivia with you in mind. She and I are old summer pals from Northeast Harbor, and there's never been anything between us but the best rapport. It occurred to me that she might be just what the doctor would order for you."

"And what gave you that idea?"

"I thought she might civilize you. She's too good and too clever for you to dismiss her in that scornful way you do most of the girls of your background. And too physically attractive not to grab an old lecher like you."

"So that's what there's in it for me. What's in it for her? Isn't there bigger game at home? Aren't there any Drexels or Biddles available?"

"I think she needs more of a challenge. I'll miss my guess if she doesn't want to lead the truculent Robin Belknap around the ring of her admirers with a ring through his nose."

Well, that was pretty much what she accomplished, despite the warning given by my friend. I fell in love with Olivia, and she returned my feeling, at least to the extent to which she was capable, which had its limits. We met every weekend in New York, New Haven or Philadelphia, and I found her exuberantly willing to share whatever activity I suggested, from sailing on Long Island Sound to taking roller-coaster rides in Coney Island. She was never tired, never in low spirits. She was willing to neck, even enthusiastically, but she firmly resisted any effort on my part to promote greater intimacy. She did not resent it, however; she regarded it as conduct to be expected of a male but to be checked by a *jeune fille à marier*, as she put it, only half-mockingly, in French.

I had the prospect of a good job in a bank that was a client of my father's firm, and when I proposed that we marry right after my Yale graduation, she agreed, but I found that she could be very definite about her conditions.

"There are certain things that you and I will have to get straight," she informed me. "I sense in you, dear, a tendency toward independence, toward your own values in life as opposed to those of the world in which you were reared." Her tone was decisive but not prim; she was trying to be fair—I see that now. She always tried to be fair. "Don't misunderstand me. I don't give a hoot about what you believe in or don't believe in. Creeds don't exist for me. You could be an atheist or an anarchist, for all I care, as long as you don't scream it from the rooftops. Or a nudist, as long as you don't make me go to a nudist camp. I expect to lead an ordered life centered in one civilized place. New York will suit me fine, if we have a decent apartment in an area of good private schools and neighbors who aren't drunks or weirdos."

"Well, that sounds reasonable enough. We'll live, in other words, as we've always lived."

"Precisely. I just want to make sure that you won't suddenly tell me we're moving to Kalamazoo. I want a solid home, a faithful husband and well-brought-up children."

"Isn't that what every true American girl wants?"

"You needn't be sarcastic, deary. The difference is that this girl means to get it."

I should have realized then that I was up against a woman of steel who would never be deflected so much as an inch from her chosen path. But I construed her open and amiable manner as a manifest of her primary devotion to me, and so we were married.

For three years things went along well enough. I was content with my work in the investment counsel department of my bank, which I did competently enough. Olivia was a cheerful and even-tempered mate, amused by the mild social gatherings of our mutual friends, always ready to go to a movie, play or concert, or to sit home with a detective story if I had to work late. Our quarrels were few and slight, and it didn't bother me that she took less interest in my philosophic or sociological opinions than she had done before we were married. I reflected that she was not, after all, gifted with a particularly interesting mind and that she had little to add to or to stimulate my thinking on questions not concerned with our daily or family life. But it was beginning to concern me that such things scarcely existed for her.

A greater problem lay in our sex life. It wasn't that Olivia failed to be willing, even a vigorous partner in this, and two sons were born to us in the first three years of our marriage. Nor was it that she took the view of some of her contemporaries (more, of course, in her mother's generation) that lovemaking was a male prerogative to which a dutiful spouse had patiently to submit. No, Olivia participated fully in our intercourse, but—how shall I put it?—in a curiously dispassionate way, as if, for hygienic purposes, she were engaged in a regular calisthenic. This ultimately diminished my libido to the point where I became a mere Saturday night performer. Olivia never commented on this.

And then came the war. Olivia thought I should go in the navy, like most of our friends, but I preferred what I fancied the "real thing": shooting at men you could see or engaging in hand-to-hand fighting, rather than firing at boats. This was again the angry, the truculent side of my nature, perhaps the immature, but I can hardly leave it out of this memorandum. I became a second lieutenant, ultimately a captain, in the infantry and fought in North Africa, Italy and at last in Germany. My sons know all about my war record and Silver Star, so I needn't go into that. What I have to stress here is what combat did to my character and personality.

It is often said that there are men who actually like war,

not just the skillful planning and execution of military strikes but the bloody filthy combat itself. I don't say that was true of me—I had my moments of hell, and I don't use that word carelessly—but I also had my moments of undoubted brute ecstasy. I had learned at boarding school to be ashamed of my impulses toward violence, but the war seemed to be offering me a vindication. The Germans were fiends, and to punish them was not only a sacred duty; it was a blissful joy. When I tramped through their shattered homeland, there was a song in my heart.

A reaction came when I saw the devastation wrought everywhere on people who had had no voice in the making of wars and when I heard of the two terrible bombs on Japan. I wondered if, had I been born in Tokyo or Berlin, I wouldn't have sprung to arms as enthusiastically as any Japanese or German youth. I began to see the whole war less as a crusade against evil and more as a sharp statement of the wretched human condition. I looked back at my appetite for battle as something sickening, and I found myself in the grip of a severe depression.

Everyone at home was most sympathetic and understanding. The bank welcomed me back; Olivia was all soothing smiles; the old friends and relatives treated me as a hero. But nothing was quite right. My two sons regarded me as something of an intruder on a home settled to suit themselves; my work at the office bored me; and Olivia, after the first year of peace, showed definite signs of impatience that I was taking so long to "snap out of it." What she particularly minded was my inclination to be silent and sometimes morose at dinner parties, and it did not lift my spirits to note with what forced gaiety and laughter she sought to counteract my dull effect on the evening cheer. Indeed, she often became the life of the party, and I could well imagine the departing guests confiding in one another about that "poor lovely woman" and wondering why she had thrown herself away on that "dreary crank."

It was inevitable that what then came into my life should have come, and I met Cornelia Tate at one of those dinner parties to the revelry of which I so scantly contributed. She was a fine woman, large and still and calm, in some ways like Olivia, but far less animated, and her large, serene gray eyes bespoke her indifference to the trivialities around her without implying the least condemnation of them or condescension. She lived, one could infer, in a world of her own, a world that satisfied her without making her smug. But that night she appeared to betray an interest in mine.

"They say you're hard to draw out," she began.

"Who says so?"

"Does it matter? Are you?"

"I can talk when I want to." I gazed at her for a moment. "I think I might like to talk to you."

"Let's try, then. Where shall we begin? Well, why not with where we are now? You hate this party, don't you?"

"Yes, and so do you. Isn't that it? Why did you come? I came because my wife brought me. Did a mate drag you here? And, by the way, which is he?"

"He's not here. We've separated, actually. I live childless and alone, and I go out when I'm asked—which is not often—because I'm afraid of getting too fond of loneliness. One can, you know. Or don't you?"

"Is it such a vice?"

"Anything can be, I suppose, if carried too far. Your adopted air—will it offend you if I call it moodiness, or semi-truculence?—might lead you down some unexpected paths."

"Such as?"

"Well, you probably think it makes you unpopular."

"And it doesn't?"

"Not with women. Your remoteness, your air of inaccessibility, may have a Byronic aspect to some. Added to your reputation as a war hero."

"What guff! Anyway, I think Olivia doesn't find it so."

"But she knows very well that others may. Oh, she keeps an eye on you!"

I looked at Cornelia with greater interest. "Does my Byronic air, as you quaintly put it, find grace with you?"

Her answer was flat. "Yes, Mr. Belknap, it does."

The conversation at the table at this point became general, and I had no further opportunity to chat with Cornelia alone, but when I called her the next day from my office and suggested that we have lunch, she immediately agreed. At the restaurant of my choice, one where we would not be likely to be seen by anyone of my acquaintance, I learned that she was a free-lance writer who reviewed books and hoped to make a name for herself with a novel that she was composing about her girlhood as a missionary's daughter in the Far East. Her husband was a lawyer in town from whom she had parted on amicable terms. She was the easiest person to talk to I had ever known, including my mother. She was perfectly willing to follow with utter frankness in any direction our colloquy pointed. She seemed afraid of nothing.

When our friendship, formed over several such lunches,

matured, as we both obviously wanted, into an affair, our noontime trysts at her garden apartment in the Village, blessed with a separate entrance, were frequent, eminently satisfactory and utterly secret. I had no wish to hurt Olivia, and Cornelia professed an interest only in the immediate present. We had no plans; we were both, as I saw it, properly civilized individuals. But she cared more than I knew. And so, perhaps, did I.

Everyone benefited from our affair. My temper improved, as did my work at the bank; I got on much better with Olivia, who was delighted at what she termed my "pulling out of it"; and I spent more time with my little boys. And Cornelia maintained that her novel, which had had its sticky points, was now progressing smoothly. When Olivia and I went out to dinner parties, where we sometimes met Cornelia, I joined in the general mirth of the evening. Life smiled.

Until Olivia found out. How did she? From a typewritten anonymous letter. She has never to this day discovered who wrote it, and when I learned who it was, I could hardly believe it. It was my mother. I had told her of my affair in one of our deep confidential discussions, because that was the kind of relationship we had, and I trusted her discretion absolutely. But when my divorce proceedings took a nasty turn, particularly in the questions of alimony and custody of the children, Mother was stricken with remorse and made her confession to me.

"I had no idea you'd be so forward in justifying what you'd done!" she protested after a fit of tears. "It never occurred to me that you'd scandalize the court by championing free sex!"

"I didn't. Olivia got hold of my correspondence with Newt Chandler and gave it to her lawyer."

"It's the same thing! How was I to know that you and he

were writing letters about your unconventional notions? I merely expected that the awful Olivia would get a common or garden type of divorce and that my darling boy would then be able to marry the woman he loved."

"I never knew you felt that way about Olivia."

"Because I took care that you shouldn't. After all, there she was, your wedded wife, and you showed no sign of being ready to shed her—not until I learned that you'd finally met a woman who understood you and loved you. Oh, I loathed Olivia from the beginning! I loathed her because I saw that she was what I'd been, a castrating female. You needn't stare at me like that. You've always thought I castrated your father. But I was determined that I'd make it up to you by never touching your manhood. You were going to be a complete man, *my* man, if there was anything I could do about it. And then that bossy Olivia had to get her claws on you!"

"But what induced you to stoop to such a thing as an anonymous letter? So unlike you, Mother!"

"Because I remembered how moral you could be about your obligation to others. I knew you'd never upset Olivia by asking for a divorce. The only way you'd get your freedom would be if *she* asked for hers! I counted on her pride and her temper and her greed. If she got everything she wanted, she'd be willing enough to let you go. Only I never thought she'd get as much as she did!"

Which, of course, was my fault. When Olivia followed up the tip of Mother's anonymous letter by hiring a detective to confirm its allegations and then faced me angrily with his report, I defended myself, claiming I had done her no wrong. Had I groveled before her as she demanded, she might have forgiven me, but when she heard my argument in rebuttal, her fury knew no bounds.

She sued for divorce in New York on the grounds of adultery, which I did not contest, and then asked for custody of our boys on the grounds that my correspondence with Newt, which she had purloined from my desk, revealed a moral character unfit to be trusted with the rearing of children. This I contested, but did not deny any item of my individual creed. I ended up with the scantest visitation rights and the loss of three-quarters of my income.

The only good thing to come out of the whole mess is that I can now marry Cornelia when she obtains the divorce that her easygoing husband will not deny her.

"And *then* we shall see," she assured me with a smile that was nothing if not enigmatic, "how *I* will behave when you find your next girl."

"Will you be another Olivia?"

"Much worse. For I shall kill you."

Nearer Today

The Treacherous Age

SOME SAY that a woman's dangerous age is forty; for me it was delayed by a decade. I had already lived half a century by the year 2000, having entered the world early in Harry Truman's second term, and on my birthday I thought, to put it as boldly as I then dared to, that I had obtained just about everything that my world had to offer.

What were those things? Well, to being with, I was a successful decorator, and had been the subject of feature articles in *Vogue* and *Architectural Digest.* My work, noted for its nostalgic return to Edwardian and late Victorian models, was reputed to be relieved from the stuffiness of pomposity of such eras by my eye for color and light and chintz, by my sense of space and air and cheerfulness, and my hand has been seen in some of the finest rooms in New York, Greenwich and the Hamptons. My husband, Augustus (Gus) Barker, to whom I have been harmoniously wed for twenty-six years, was a member of Harrison Levy, internationally known investment bankers, and made a fortune of I don't even know how many millions. We lived in a splendid penthouse on Park Avenue and a thirty-room "cottage" on the beach in Southampton. Our two children were happily and substantially married, my daughter to a junior partner of her father's and my son to the daughter of a former governor of New York. I had managed to preserve both my health and my figure, was considered an exceptionally handsome woman for my age and had once been listed in *Style* magazine among the ten best-dressed women in Manhattan.

So why have I been struck by a nagging little doubt that has grown as rapidly as a malignant tumor and landed me at the gates of a nervous breakdown? I've tried to attribute it to advancing age, to a delayed change in life, to a puritan sense of having been too long the darling of fate, or to some inevitable rebalancing of scales tipped too far in my favor, but I keep coming back to one thing: my marriage.

Not that Gus has become in any way uncongenial or been unfaithful or deficient in expressed affection. In everything we have done together, he has always had my full concurrence. Let me try to put it this way: he created me. Or, better yet, he fitted me into the setting of his life as adroitly and seamlessly as a great stage director might fit a vital prop into the scenery of his drama. Now what's wrong with that if the show succeeds? And ours has succeeded—you might say, with standing room only. Aren't I the beneficiary as well as he? Ah, yes, but it is always *his* show, never mine. I have a life, yes, and what many would call a very good one, but is it mine? Can I say that I have really lived?

The psychiatrist whom I have consulted suggested that it might help me—and her—if I wrote up a short summary of what I considered the salient facts of my biography, which, of course, is what I am doing now. In novels and short stories this kind of exercise is made interesting if the reader is able to note passages where the writer is evidently under a delusion, or where he or she is consciously or unconsciously altering facts to justify or vindicate past doings. But there will be no reader of this memorandum unless I decide to show it to the doctor who suggested its preparation. I cannot be sure that I am always telling the truth, but I can certainly be sure that I am trying to, for it would be curiously foolish to pick up my pen in order to fool myself. Yet people do it, one knows. In any case, I must make a start.

I was born Alida Schuyler, to a younger branch of the great clan that Lyman Horace Weeks designated, in his *Prominent Families of New York*, "one of the most distinguished in the United States." The ambitious and "upwardly mobile" Alexander Hamilton had chosen his bride from a senior branch as a way to cloak his illegitimate birth. Through the generations, we replenished our diminishing coffers by marrying into the families of the new and newer rich, and few young men started life with more advantages than my father, who had good looks, money and a venerable name—Livingston (Livy) Van Rensselaer Schuyler—though it sounded like the take-off of an old New York moniker in a Harvard Hasty Pudding show. But what good could all that do a man if he was born an ass?

That was the question I put to myself again and again as early as the age of sixteen, as I watched our fortune dribbled away by Daddy in such ill-advised investments as gaudy "epic" movies and awkwardly situated amusement parks, lured by big-talking touts who hopped cheerfully from bankruptcy to bankruptcy until they finally hit the jackpot—after leaving Daddy far behind. They gambled for the fun of it, but Daddy did it to make money, which is always fatal. When he was reduced to a small but life-saving trust fund that he couldn't invade, he retired from business to divide his life between the golf course and the bridge table, at both of which he excelled and to which he should have devoted himself from the beginning.

Mother, beautiful, languid and of simpler origins, (Daddy, unlike his wiser forebears, had married for love), thought she would have no further trouble in life after she became Mrs. Schuyler, but when the unrestricted money was gone, she showed herself unexpectedly efficient in taking control of the trust income—Daddy had been shamed into submission—and using it with enough dexterity, plus her sagacity in cadging favors from rich friends and relations, to preserve a niche for her family on the fringe of the "best" society. Huddling under its precarious covers, she may even have felt a species of happiness.

Such content, if content it was, was not for me. I had observed my parents' world critically and assessed its value—accurately, I think. It still had some of the old trimmings of its former high status; few of its members had fared financially as disastrously as my father; a goodly number were richer than their parents had been. What happened to them was simply that they lost their monopoly; their clubs and private schools and exclusive resorts were not taken from them but had now to be shared with those once rejected. There was enough money for both old and new rich, though the new appeared to have the lion's share of it, and no one was more conscious of the destiny of that share than Miss Alida Schuyler. I realized that my name was no longer an honor card, but it was still a card, and you can win a trick with the two of clubs if it's a trump. It's a question of playing every pasteboard in your hand for its maximum value. My parents exhausted all the mental skill they had at the bridge table. I preferred a larger sphere of action.

The nineteen-sixties were the period of my greatest revelation. At Spence School in New York and at boarding school in Farmington, Connecticut, I was a docile and conventional student, with my eyes open and my criticism suppressed. I always felt not only that I was at odds with most of the people around me, but that any protest I enunciated would fall on deaf and perhaps scandalized ears. My parents, as I have indicated, were frozen in the glacial past of their imagination, and many of the boys and girls of my age, particularly the latter, were living in the future, equally unreal, of theirs. They exulted in the prediction that a new age was dawning, one where the old rules of sexual propriety, class distinction, formality of dress, religious observance and patriotism would be swept aside in favor of freedom of choice and act, freedom, in short, of everything. This was accompanied, of course, by the reign of drugs, and it may have been the violent and prolonged attack of nausea that followed my first and only experiment with marijuana that proved my salvation. What I gleaned from the experience was the knowledge that my contemporaries could prove themselves just as silly asses as my parents, and that was my first step to maturity.

When my older sister ran off with a young man under a suspended sentence for passing drugs, and had to be recovered by the payment to her vile seducer of a sum my parents could ill afford, I made my definitive break with this "wave of the future." I would prepare myself to succeed in a world that was neither my sister's nor my parents'—in other words, *the* world.

It seemed to me that all the protests against the war in Vietnam had only hardened the grim obstinacy of misguided hawks and that the goal of new liberties had only betrayed our youthful extremists into the clutches of anarchists and Reds. When the great breaker of the new wave finally broke, what was left but free sex? And how can you make a life or a living out of that? While, in the meantime, all around us were rising the new millionaires.

I took to reading articles about the luxuriously appointed interiors of the new—and old—rich in the fashion magazines and decided that therein lay my future—or my beginning. Mother entirely approved of my choice, as decorating was the most acceptable of ladies' occupations, and she arranged for my interview with the man who became the first great teacher and influence in my life, Beverly Bogardus.

He was then in his mid-thirties, a decade and a half older than I, and already a rising star in the decorating world. He took an immediate interest in me as soon as he learned—for I at once felt that I could be frank with him—that I was totally uncommitted to any political or social change in the world about me. He hired me, though at an exiguous salary, and, in developing my own style, I took more than a few hints from his. He was certainly something of a genius in his field. He could make a future out of the past while shunning the banality of the modern. What I think he saw in me was a Schuyler saved from the terrible sixties, a Schuyler, so to speak, unspoiled, who could be used in shaping a future as yet undetermined.

He was not, by any means, a handsome man. He had a long, lanky figure and a sloppy posture, and his messy blond hair fell down over a wizened pale countenance with large, unexpectedly boyish blue eyes, which lent him briefly an air of youthful innocence that was entirely misleading. He was brilliantly sardonic and utterly without mercy in his assessments of even close friends, but there never seemed any bile or ill temper in the cheerful guffaws that his own sallies evoked from him. He mocked himself as well as the world, or gave the impression of doing so.

The reason, I learned early, that he never attained the first position in our profession was that he would never put himself out for people. He was notoriously slow in his work, and not even the shrillest protest of the richest châtelaine would induce him to accelerate the completion of one of her chambers. He would absent himself from the office for days at a time without offering so much as a lame excuse. He acted as if he despised his success as sincerely as he did that of his rivals. He was widely supposed to be homosexual, and I had reason to believe that his strong attachment to my husband, though not returned in the same way, was more than platonic, but he was also known to have been the lover of a great society beauty. I believe he was attracted by the unattainable, in both sexes. Or it may have been that he disdained to commit himself to any bourgeois limitation in the areas of sexual gratification. He would never have lost the world for love, or lost love for the world.

He paid closer attention to me and my training than he did to any other junior in his office, and he sometimes described me to friends, only half-mockingly, as a Trilby to his Svengali. But he was interested in teaching me more than the art of design. He wanted me to understand the workings of our world, and he professed to see, in the increased lavishness of the homes of the rich—the meat and drink of our business—not the mere icing on the cake of a material society, but the heart and soul of a desperately corrupted era.

"Read Balzac," he urged me. "His human comedy is our own. His France of the Bourbon restoration saw its political left and political right both hit the dust before the onslaught of a united bourgeoisie. The left had been discredited by the Reign of Terror; the right by its intransigent clinging to a feudal past. As with us! Our left has been discredited by its long subjection to Stalinism and our right by its outdated faith in economic laissez-faire. So the goldbugs have swarmed in to fill a yawning vacuum. We wanted a world where every man would earn a living wage. Well, we have it. In the Great Depression of the thirties a man would carry a pike in the grand march in *Aida* for a buck a night; today, he has to have a minimum wage, Social Security and unemployment and perhaps medical insurance. But that costs money, and where are you going to get it? Not from Reds or bureaucrats or economists, but from goldbugs. So goldbugs rule the world!"

"Why do you tell me all this?" I asked at one of our protracted lunches. His never took less than two hours. "You can't think that I'll make a fortune. Surely not of our lampshades and chintzes."

"No, my dear, but you might marry one."

And of course it was Beverly who introduced me to my husband. He and Gus Barker had been roommates at Columbia College, and their friendship was lifelong. Yet they were as close to being diametric opposites as is possible for two men to be. Gus was lean and strong and wiry with a dark complexion, shiny black hair and a habitual expression of being neither fooled nor impressed, only of dispassionately assessing a person or situation. He was not strikingly handsome; his black eyes were too close together and his head a trifle too thin, but his supple movements and well-sculpted torso gave him the agility of a fine feline. I felt with him the force of a perfectly adjusted male, one who could take you apart, if necessary, and put you back together without a single part missing or out of place.

He was already rich when Beverly introduced us, a junior partner in his famous firm, and educated entirely, I gathered, at public schools and at Columbia on a competitively earned scholarship. His background was obscure; it was much later that I learned that his father had been a New York City cop. I gathered that most of his relatives were dead; he certainly did not deny their existence or hide them, for he was ashamed of nobody, but it was clear that he was alone in the world. It would have been impossible for even a keen observer to fit him into a particular social class; his easy self-confidence and quiet good manners made him at home in any group.

The very first time he took me out, after our introduction by the casually sly Beverly, it was apparent, though not through any clumsy ogle or untoward remark, that he was looking me over as a candidate for a serious role in his busy life, undoubtedly at the suggestion of his old college chum.

At the French restaurant where he competently and briefly ordered our expensive dinner and a noble wine, I asked him, as my few close girlfriends always advised, about his business, which he disposed of with a few modest comments. But when I contrasted his success with my father's poor record, he became more illuminating.

"Your father has been the victim of the foolish American creed that a man must always do something. Though he inherited enough money to live comfortably, he had to go to work to increase it. That often results in a man's losing it. There are plenty of men, good men too, who can't afford to work. If your father had spent his days stretched out on the sand at Palm Beach, he'd be a rich man today."

"You think that's all he's good for," I retorted defensively.

"Not at all. A talent for gain is only one talent in a man, but it's a necessary one in the money game. With too many of our tycoons it's the only one they have. They have no idea what to do with the money once they've earned it."

"They leave that to their families."

"Unfortunately, they often do. But your father could have done lots of other things. Charities and trusteeships and saving the environment ..."

I broke in. "And collecting button hooks?"

"Why not?"

"He plays a very good game of bridge."

"Well, that's something, isn't it? The great thing is to do well whatever you're doing."

"What will you do? When your pile of Rhinegold is high enough to hide Freia from the giants and your youth is given back to you?"

"That remains to be seen. But I trust that I'll do it well."

I could see from the first date that Gus was determined to have everything in the world, and I had my first glimmer that I was destined to be a part of that everything. But I had no idea of resenting it then. It seemed to me, both before and after our marriage, that he assessed me at my exact worth. He took my decorating seriously, holding to the modern idea that a woman should have a career, and grateful that I hadn't chosen the drabber occupation of lawyer or accountant, which might have interfered with the role I was to play as consort to an international and widely traveling investment banker. Nor was I to engage in Veblen's "conspicuous consumption." Though I was always to be dressed well—and his sharp eye censored my wardrobe—I was also, even on business trips, to be a "real" decorator; and many, if not most, of my best jobs were commissioned by the wives of his business associates.

Oh, yes, there was to be nothing fake about the "lovely Mrs. Gus Barker." I was to be like everything else in his life, the genuine article. Even my ancestry was to be tastefully and never brazenly demonstrated. The Schuyler family portraits that Gus purchased from impecunious cousins were handsome works of art in themselves and were hung in inconspicuous but appropriate corners of our apartment, not pompously displayed in the hall or over a principal fireplace.

And so in a surprisingly short number of years we reached the top, or what he and I and his mighty partners—how can I separate myself from them?—considered the top. There was a pleasant tinge of the liberal in our entourage, for Gus, who did not believe that either of our two major political parties had much effect on the thrust of our surging economy, found it more "attractive" to hunt with the Democrats rather than with their more flat-footed opponents. This helped with our children, who were never able to get a toehold in the slippery elevation of their father's apparently liberal philosophy to stage the rebellion so craved by many of their contemporaries and finally dropped back into a decorous and well-rewarded submission.

So there I was, seated on the veranda of our big, cool,

spotlessly white house on the Southampton dunes, or gazing over Manhattan from the huge windows of our penthouse, an integral part of a matchless setting. Gus's bathroom in the apartment, faced north, toward the George Washington Bridge; sitting on his john, he could see all the kingdoms of the world as if they were being offered to him by Satan. But didn't he own them already? What could he do but shit on them?

Ah, you see, I churn with bitterness. It was, in fact, Beverly who said that to me, but he was looking at me with that horrid little smile that showed he'd read my thoughts. He had stopped by that morning for a pre-luncheon glass of sherry and had excused himself to go to the bathroom. Knowing his way about the apartment, he had gone to Gus's and, struck again by the panorama before him, had summoned me to recall the scene of Christ's temptation.

It was at that moment I conceived the idea that Beverly had only the lowest opinion of Gus's material success, that he actually despised it. It may strike one as odd that I had not thought of this before, since nobody knew better than I that Beverly was the classic underachiever—as a collector, critic, even as a decorator—and that his principal joy was sneering at the world. But I had clung to my faith that Gus was the one exception to his rule, that he admired (and adored) my husband as the one man whose life and thinking made a kind of dignified sense in a universe of cant.

And after that day I started to notice, at first in light shades but soon in more pronounced colors, the development of a new aspect of Beverly's personality in his relationship with my husband. He was becoming a proselyter for the arts. Gus, in the eyes of Beverly, had conquered Mammon, a minor victory;

now it behooved him to move on to the nobler field of the arts, to seek his salvation, so to speak, at the altar of man-created beauty.

Soon Gus and I were passing pleasant Saturday afternoons touring the art galleries of Fifty-seventh Street and SoHo in the company of the knowledgeable Beverly, and Gus found himself buying oils, watercolors and prints under his friend's expert supervision. As my husband always did things on a large scale and was inclined to be impatient in his eagerness to follow up any new enthusiasm, it was not long before the walls of our apartment could boast of an impressive collection of abstract expressionists.

But was it so impressive? I began to wonder that after Gus's purchase, for a smacking sum, of an oil that was a square of thickly painted inky black. Beverly had airily represented it as the ultimate of some extremist school, but many of my friends laughed at it; one of them suggested it was a school blackboard. And then Gus went in for a series of sketches of lines and squiggles that looked to me like the doodlings of a bored director at a dull corporate meeting. And after that he acquired a score of paintings of colored bars, some arranged in parallel fashion as in a flag and others in concentric circles like archery targets. At last, when the delivery men from a famous gallery unpacked in my presence a huge black and white canvas that depicted what looked like a cross between a menacing praying mantis and the skeleton of a skyscraper under construction, I allowed myself to speculate that the omniscient Beverly was making sly fun of us. Did it amuse his idle fancy to see how far an innocent tycoon could be pushed?

And there was another change in Beverly's attitude toward

my husband, one that struck me as sinister. I've already indicated that Gus had shown a definite but hardly overwhelming interest in my Schuyler ancestry. And recently he had shown a new concern about allying himself more closely with members of New York's old Knickerbocker society or what was left of it. He joined the Hone Club, for whose stuffy conservatism he and Beverly had once had nothing but sneers, and he improved his horsemanship by taking lessons in jumping, preparatory to joining a fox hunt in northern New Jersey. Beverly, of course, was quick to make sarcastic note of all this.

One morning when I was showing him the almost perfect copy of a French eighteenth-century *fauteuil* that Gus, without consulting either Beverly or me, had ordered for his study, Beverly burst out in a tone that had little of the underpinning of affection he habitually used in speaking of my husband: "Prerevolutionary Gaul is the eternal trap of the *bourgeois gentilhomme*. Almost anything else can be copied, but *it* must be genuine, and that's what the new rich can never see. The Wrightsmans, of course, are exceptions, and what they've done for the Metropolitan is magnificent. But this piece—no. And while we're on the point, you may warn our dear Augustus of the dangers of too close an adherence to the aristocratic standards of the stately past. Nor need you penetrate further than your own family history. I cite only the example of the illustrious Alexander Hamilton, who sought to cover a bastard birth with a Schuyler spouse but lost his life by conforming to what he wrongly considered a gentleman's code of honor. Only a parvenu at that late date in the history of New York would have decided that Burr's affront mandated a duel to the death!"

I did not like this; I did not like it at all. For his tone was not only contemptuous; it sounded cruel. It was hard to accept that he was speaking of his dearest friend.

It was probably this note that prepared me for what I was to consider the ultimate revelation of something like a master plan on Beverly's part. A master plan but a kind of devil's work. It was his inducing Gus to invest a spanking sum of money in an avant-garde production of *Othello* by one of Beverly's young theatrical protégés.

The tragedy was performed in modern dress, and every character was represented as gay except Othello, and there evidently was some doubt about him in the malevolent mind of Iago. The latter's motivation, of course, was his unreturned passion for the big muscular black and his misogynist compulsion to rid the world of his rival, Desdemona. The direction was awkward; the actors ranted, and the production failed after seventeen performances. But it gave me proof, if proof were needed, that Beverly, as a modern Iago, was stirred, not as in Coleridge's famous phrase, by "motiveless malignity," but by a fierce inner need to bring my husband down.

Why? Who knew? Because Gus had never loved him as he loved Gus? Because Gus loved me—or, at any rate, slept with me but not him? Or because Gus was a strong man beyond the debilitating weakness of love, and he, Beverly, was racked with jealousy and hate? Or simply because Gus was a great success in the world, and Beverly, for all his pretended detachment, sorely resented his relative obscurity? Was a decorator, after all, no matter how esteemed, a real man? Or his success a real success?

After mulling over my theory heatedly for a few days, I came to a desperate decision. Why should I not take the bull by the horns and show this memorandum to Beverly? He might only indulge in one of his long, sneering laughs; he might fly into one of his very rare but very violent tantrums; he might even show the memo scornfully to Gus (which I didn't at all wish); but in any case he would abort or drastically revise his campaign of denigration. I should have the relief of at least a temporary truce.

It is done. I have mailed him a copy of this paper without a covering note.

I suppose I should have expected this answer from one so clever.

> My dear Alida,
>
> How neatly you have transferred all your resentment of your noble spouse to the fortunately broad shoulders of his ever loyal friend! Because you cannot bear the idea of his having catapulted you into a fame and fortune you would never have achieved on your own, you crave the revenge of turning him into an ass and laying the blame on the one human being who has consistently loved and appreciated him and tried to guide him in those rare fields in which he needed something besides his own strong will and genius. In art, I have helped him to assemble the finest examples of such great lights as Barnett Newman, Cy Twombly, Kenneth Noland and Franz Kline; and in the theater, his name has been associated with a Shakespearean revival that, if a box office failure, has been acclaimed by the cognoscenti. Look into your heart, dear girl, and recognize that you have suffered only what lesser souls suffer when they are

associated with larger ones, and be grateful that you did not wed one lesser than yourself!

I hate Beverly Bogardus! But I am still not going to show this memorandum to my doctor.

The Merger

IN 1970, still in his early fifties and looking forward to at least a decade, if not considerably more, of his brilliantly successful career as president, CEO and board chairman (the triple title settled any question of who was boss) of New Hampshire Wire and Cable, Gary Kimball faced the first serious attack on his leadership. And it was not from an outside raider or from one of the frustrated labor unions with which he had once been in battle. No, the onslaught came from the bosom of his own family.

It was time for him, sitting in his lofty office in the Empire State Building, the center of his worldwide operations, to review his life and determine where he had gone wrong—if indeed he had gone wrong. He had obviously first to face his lifelong preoccupation with the family business, founded and controlled by his late father, whose favorite and favored son he had been, a preoccupation that had made the role in his life of the other family members, particularly after his father's demise and the division of his stock among them, quite as much that of shareholders as of blood kin. But had he not moved mountains to keep them rich and happy?

His father, Alonso Kimball, had been a gentle kindly man of the highest moral integrity, with the strict old-fashioned principles that required a gentleman to pay his father's debts as though they were his own, regardless of the cost to himself or his family, and who indeed had done so, delaying by several years the making of his fortune. He had responded enthusiastically to Gary's early fascination with the source of the family wealth and had made a practice, waving aside his wife's protests, of taking Gary along with him, no matter what school schedule had to be interrupted, on his frequent inspections of the company's plants in different states. Away from the rather hothouse atmosphere of the Fifth Avenue apartment where Gary's mother, to his youthful mind, "lolled" amid a profusion of flowers and French eighteenth-century furnishings, or the well-mowed lawns and cultivated gardens of the Westchester estate, the boy found what he called a more "real" reality in the hard shining objects that the great whirring machinery of his father's factories produced: blades, knives, tools of every kind that bit or pinched or shoveled or squeezed, huge hoists of cable or wire, scissors, scalpels, vises, hammers, saws, bolts and keys, down to the very simplicity of button hooks and paper clips. Bright luminous things, things that lasted, not flabby things, not things that grew fat and soft and decayed, like human flesh. Ugh!

The intimate and lasting relationship that Gary developed with his father set them somewhat apart from the rest of the family, from his tall, pale, gracious, art-loving and salon-presiding mother, his merry, pretty, flirtatious sister, May, and his charming but epicurean kid brother, Gilbert. It was not that any of these three was jealous of Gary's taking over the head of the household. Papa, of course, was an "old darling"; Papa was always buying them the most wonderful things; but Papa was more absorbed in his business than anything else. Papa, if they faced it squarely, was something of a bore, and if Gary amused him and kept his sharp eye from too close an inspection of their romps at home, well, that was all to the good.

Gary grew into a serious lad of a slight but well-formed build and a pale and impassive countenance, with small regular features and thick dark hair he wore in a crewcut. What people noticed particularly about him were his eyes, which tended to stare, taking in the onlooker without betraying any hint of the judgment formed. And at Chelton, the Massachusetts Episcopal boarding school, of which his father was a trustee and where he spent his four pre-Harvard years, he was essentially a solitary student.

It was not that he was unpopular or deficient in athletics or grades. He got on well enough with the other boys, largely because of his habit of quietly conforming to the school routine, which he saw no reason to oppose. He performed adequately if unremarkably in his classes and sports, and he hardly received a black mark or demerit in conduct throughout his four years at the school. But as one master remarked to his father, "Gary has an air of not being quite here." By "here," of course, he meant at Chelton. Alonso Kimball had smiled to himself. He knew where the boy's mind was. It was where his own was: in the terrible struggle the family company was having to survive the dark years of the Depression that had followed the stock market collapse of 1929.

The placid red-bricked and white-columned school buildings encircling a shimmering green, elm-studded lawn might have seemed remote from unemployment and poverty, but Gary was acutely aware of formerly rich boys who were suddenly put on scholarships and others who had to leave school altogether, and he pored over the long letters in which his father explained, in the same detail he would have to a business partner, his tireless and ultimately successful battle to bring his company through the tangled thicket of a prolonged economic crisis that, in Alonso's fixed opinion, had been aggravated and not abated by the advent of the New Deal. The paternal triumph, of which Gary had never seriously doubted, served to convince the boy of the rightness of his father's lifelong creed: that capitalism, free and unregulated, was the answer to all the ills of mankind. Alonso's remedy for the Depression would have been to allow the stock market to hit bottom, if that was its natural tendency, at which point the recuperative powers innate in the system would have begun to operate and revive it. Any interference could come only from the devil, who began to take on a likeness in Alonso's imagination to the Hudson River squire who so jauntily sought to steer the rocking and heaving ship of state.

One spring there was a bad forest fire in the neighborhood of the school, and several hundred young men from the Civilian Conservation Corps were called in to help the local firefighters. Chelton's headmaster volunteered to send in his older students to lend what aid they could, and Gary found himself assigned to an unburning but threatened area to await the onslaught of the flames, which in fact never came, as the fire was brought under control. But Gary, sitting around in the company of these young men and listening to their casually obscene chatter, had his first experience with lower-class American adult males, and they did not impress him. What could you do with such people? A fascist state would arm them, and they would become killers; a socialist or communist one would give them everything, and they would bankrupt the land. Only a capitalist state could cope with them; they would all go to work and be told how to do it. Perish by guns or starve under bureaucrats; those were the alternatives to an economy run by free enterprise.

There was a great deal of religion dished up for the boys at Chelton, but Gary had no personal use for it. It might be a handy thing to keep the lower orders quiet—pie in the sky if none on earth—and it was manifestly unwise and unproductive to air agnostic views on the subject. And wasn't the truth, the real truth, manifest enough even under the looming presence of the great Gothic tower of the school chapel? Who had built the chapel but a wealthy graduate? Who made up the board of trustees but successful lawyers and businessmen? Was the great God-fearing and God-imploring headmaster himself not a member of a famous banking family? And were not most of Gary's classmates headed for careers on Wall or State Street?

Every now and then a clever master would sense the implied dissent behind the silence of this grave but preoccupied student and seek to entice the boy into an exchange of ideas.

"I sometimes wonder," one of them said to Gary in the fall of his final year at school, "if Chelton doesn't have too many campus activities for sixteen- and seventeen-year-olds. Shouldn't there be more time for those on the threshold of manhood to contemplate the mystery of the universe and find their own souls?"

Gary agreed politely, but the master, baffled by his continued taciturnity, turned away and did not try again. He couldn't have known that Gary believed that he had long since found his soul.

In his college years Gary spent his vacations in his father's office or touring the factories, learning every aspect of the business. And when the war came in 1941, it wasn't difficult for Alonso, heavily engaged in supplying the armed forces with metalwork, to arrange for the assignment of his elder son, as an ensign, to the Navy Department in Washington to check munitions contracts with an eye as expert as many a trained lawyer's. So even the world crusade against Hitler and Hirohito was converted, in Gary's case, to the final chapter of his indoctrination into the world of industrial management.

The ensuing quarter-century marked the rise of the Kimball company into the first rank of metal suppliers. It was Gary, always at his father's right hand, who devised the solution to the constantly recurring clashes with labor: move the plants south in search of poorer and more submissive workers, or out of the country altogether, to Korea, to Guatemala, to South Africa, to Bolivia. Alonso showed some reluctance at first, but the immediate benefits, so easing to his old habits of worry, his increasing age, with its attendant ailments, and his pride in his brilliant son, soon quelled his patriotic doubts about hiring so few Americans to do the work of an American business. And after his death, following a long illness, Gary reigned supreme, with no one in management to criticize or question his policies.

But the year 1970 brought a horrid surprise: a long, well-researched and vividly illustrated *New York Times* article on "slave labor" in a Kimball plant in Guatemala. It was followed by a brief flap of public indignation and a mild effort to boycott some of the products of New Hampshire Wire and Cable.

Gary chose to ignore the whole matter and refused to give interviews or to answer press telephone calls, but he could not avoid a meeting at his mother's apartment with her and Nicholas Gilder, husband of his sister, May.

Of course, it was Nick who had talked Gary's nervous and ill-at-ease mother into this confrontation. Nick, large, handsome, outgoing, redheaded, popular everywhere, particularly in his native Boston, where he was a well-known Brahmin and vigorous yachtsman, was a notorious underachiever. He had made an unsuccessful but highly publicized run for the state senate, after which he settled back to a life of pleasure, but Gary had always been aware that his sister's husband had a large store of unused brains and energy, which Gary knew should be diverted from company affairs.

Loud, emphatic, but not unreasonable, Nick now proceeded to summarize the *Times*'s findings. He ended by demanding to know to what extent the late Alonso Kimball had been responsible for the overseas hiring policy.

"Daddy approved of everything I did," Gary replied. "From the very beginning."

"In principle, yes. But was he aware of the conditions of the workers? I can hardly believe it in a man of his humanitarian views."

"So unlike mine, you mean?" Gary, determined to control his temper, could take just so much from the man he referred to privately as "the hedonist baked bean."

"All right, Gary, so unlike you." Nick did not hesitate to take the offensive. Yet there was no anger in his tone. Indeed, there was no anger in his contempt. "I've always known your god was the dollar." He turned to his mother-in-law. "Wasn't Mr. Kimball's mind weakening in his later years?"

"Oh, yes, I'm afraid that's all too true. You know that yourself, don't you, Gary dear?"

Gary sighed with exasperation. Without Nick he could have handled his mother, but with him it was much harder. Adelaide Kimball was the kind of woman of her generation who tended in any serious discussion to favor the physically stronger and handsomer man, and he could hardly compare himself with the stalwart Nick.

"Mother, Daddy always knew everything I did!" he protested. "And his mind at the end, if it wasn't all it had been, was certainly capable of taking in the essentials of our policy. Daddy believed in free enterprise. He didn't believe in telling other nations how to run their economies. If a man in Indonesia or Burma was willing to work for less than one in Detroit or Sacramento, he would take the lower bid; that's all. I'm not breaking any law. Even any moral law. The lower wage may be the equivalent of the higher in spending power in the third world. Is it my job to lobby for a 'new deal' all over the globe?"

"Free enterprise!" exclaimed Nick scornfully. "Ask your peons in Central America how free they are!"

"Well, why haven't you looked into this before, Nick? Because you've been too busy touring the oceans in your big pleasure boat! Cruising in the South Sea islands and admiring the picturesque natives without worrying your red head about what they live on. At least I give them something. And in some cases more than they've ever had before."

"The reproach to me is not unjustified," Nick admitted, addressing his mother-in-law. "But I see now that Gary's policy is to drug us into passivity. Very clever, I must say. But hardly scrupulous."

"If you think that running a company night and day for a

quarter of a century in order to bring wealth and ease to a bunch of idlers is unscrupulous, then you're welcome to the word!"

"It's just what I do think. And I'm embarrassed to hell that it's taken me so long to find it out!"

At which Gary walked out of the meeting.

At home in his penthouse aerie, hanging over the East River, in the gleaming white drawing room—all spotless, shimmering white, except for the brackets, and arms and legs of chairs and tables, gold-tinted—he submitted to a rare impulse to seek sympathy from the wife who presided so meticulously over the perfect maintenance of their abode. Katrina's slim, trim build and crisply waved black hair lent her a chic that almost but never quite compensated for the awkward slant of her nose, her small pinched lips and those sharp dark eyes that were so ready to disapprove.

She listened with a mild impatience as he expatiated on the scene at his mother's.

"Don't those things blow over?" she commented at last. "Isn't it pretty much like the strike in the Michigan plant where that man was killed? Who remembers that now? In a month's time Nick will have gone back to his boat and your mother will be dreaming of her next pet poet or painter. Tell them you'll send someone down to Guatemala to check on the report. You might even hike the wages a couple of pesetas. Or, better yet, fire one of the managers. It shouldn't be hard to find a crooked one. Or we might go ourselves, in March, instead of to Acapulco. I hear there's a divine new hotel on the beach at San José. Betty Crunch was there and adored it." And then she turned, as if to business. "Look, dear, it's time to dress. We're dining at the Hoopers'. I thought you'd never get home."

With which she rose and left him, heading for her bedroom. He sighed. But he knew he couldn't complain. He had married exactly the wife he had wanted, and she had exactly fulfilled his expectations. She was sober, punctual and efficient; she never interfered with his long hours of work; and she had given him the requisite family, a boy and a girl, both now in proper boarding schools. Daughter of a famous banker who had killed himself when bankrupt, she had grown up resolutely determined to make a stable match and have a stable income. If she had ever suffered from a romantic urge, she had never shown it. She had been quite content to use her agile mind at the card table or in the choice of her wondrous wardrobe or in constantly redecorating her apartment and two country villas. The only remnants of her childhood bitterness were in a scowling look and in her sharp dislike of any persons whose demeanor or conversation suggested that they thought they had more substance in their lives than she.

His father had always warned Gary that his first job would be to keep the family happy. When Gary was just shy of his eighteenth birthday, on the weekend of his graduation from Chelton, Alonso, who had come up to school for the event, took him on a solemn walk to the river.

"You and I must be entirely frank with each other, dear boy. It's now pretty clear that your brother, Gilbert, is never going to develop either the head or the inclination for business, and your sister will presumably marry and have a family to constitute her primary interest. Your mother, of course, has always refused to look at an account book, much less to set foot in one of our plants. So it will all rest on your shoulders, my son. I have given you in my will as much control of the business as I can, but I cannot, of course, bypass my beloved wife, daughter and younger son, and no matter what I attempt to accomplish with voting powers in your shares, there is no way that your mother and siblings with their preponderant equity in the company, will not be able to make trouble for you, if, for some unforeseeable reason, they should take it into their heads to 'gang up on you.' To avoid this, you must keep them abreast of what's going on in the business and see to it that their dividends keep rolling in. But it shouldn't be too hard, because their attention span for monetary matters is brief, and once they trust you at the helm, they'll be only too glad to leave everything to you."

All this Gary had done, though somewhat differently in each case. Gilbert, for example, he had taken into the business. Gilbert, rosy-cheeked, blue-eyed and blond-haired, was the charming idler of the family; he had the greatest difficulty in avoiding expulsion from different institutions of learning. Gary decided to grapple with this and to rectify his brother's natural laziness by giving him the flattering job of acting as his personal assistant, which had the additional merit of keeping him under close observation. He was also careful to give Gilbert plenty of time off and a salary many times greater than he was worth. He turned his brother, in short, into the kind of aide every great man needs, one who is blindly devoted to the boss and can never become a rival. And Gilbert's generous nature made him recognize all that Gary had done for him. He became his brother's admiring slave.

Gary's mother had been easier to handle. Adelaide Kimball, as a devoted reader of Victorian fiction, had always had a sneaking sympathy for the British upper-class prejudice against people in "trade" and a horror of even hearing about the family business. To keep her happy and uninquiring, Gary had only to see that she had the funds to add to her collection of French paintings, drawings, porcelains and furniture. But he made himself something of an expert in her field to be sure that she bought things that would appreciate in value. So successful were they in partnership that Madame de Pompadour, he liked to say, returning to earth, would have found herself quite at home in Adelaide's drawing room.

His sister, May, was a high-spirited, handsome and theoretically independent woman who regarded the sexes as equal and herself fully as qualified as any man to ask and answer questions at a stockholders' meeting. But her impatience with detail made her easily bored, and Gary knew just how to use the intricacies of trade in a way to make her throw up her hands and leave everything to management, i.e., *his* management. Her husband was the real problem and the most expensive to solve. That big beautiful sailing yacht and its crew had cost Gary a pretty penny, though it would have been worth twice the sum to keep its skipper away in distant seas on expeditions undertaken for the Museum of Natural History!

And now, alas, Nick was home, with no sign of disappearing on or in the briny deep.

Gary's next step was to get hold of Gilbert before the latter was corrupted by Nick. But he found he had been forestalled. At the office the next day he was told that his brother was home with the flu, and when he telephoned, Gilbert's pretty but empty-headed little blonde of a wife, obviously nervous, informed him that Gilly was sleeping and shouldn't be disturbed. It was evident that Gilbert would do anything rather than talk to him, though he was not too ill to attend a family conference summoned by Nick at Adelaide's apartment the very next day at six.

Gary arrived to find Nick, May, his mother, Gilbert and Gilbert's wife, Sophie, already grimly assembled in the drawing room. Gilbert's expression was strained, and he avoided his brother's sharp glances.

Nick opened the meeting with a concise but accurate summary of the *Times* report, followed by a brief account of the answers he had received from an officer of the family company to questions he had put as to conditions in its plants in other countries. He ended with the suggestion that the facts were being blurred to the shareholders but that he strongly suspected things were a lot worse than the *Times* had implied, and he called for a total reconsideration of overseas hiring.

In the silence that followed, Gary kept his eyes fixed on Gilbert, and when he spoke it was to ignore his brother-in-law's oration.

"Why didn't you come to me, Gil? Why did you sit by and let Nick prepare all this garbage without a word to me?"

"Because I advised him not to!" Nick broke in angrily. "Because I knew you had him paralyzed with a false sense of what he owes you at the office. Just the way you've shell-shocked the rest of us. It's not to our credit, I fully admit. But all things have their end, and your game is up, Gary. You may as well face it."

"Nick, you're going too far," Gilbert protested, obviously in the greatest discomfort at being caught in the crossfire between Nick and his boss brother. "There's no reason we can't work these things out in a friendly and sensible fashion. And it wasn't Nick who first put me on to what we were doing abroad," he continued, turning at last to Gary. "It was my little Sophie here."

"Sophie?" Gary repeated in astonishment.

Gilbert's wife spoke up now in a flurry of shyness. "It was at a lecture I attended at the New School for Social Research. The speaker mentioned the name of your company and went on to give some appalling figures. I was so ashamed that I hid my face when I left the classroom, even though nobody knew who I was."

"Gary, my dear," his mother intervened, "I'm sure you will see to it that something is done to alleviate these appalling conditions."

"I can assure you, Mother, that I will, and please forgive me for the rude term I used to describe Nick's proposal."

He closed his eyes and his lips tightly for a second while he got hold of himself. After all, what was it but the continuation of a struggle in which he had always had the foresight and will power to win?

When he came home and described the meeting to Katrina, it was immediately apparent that, unlike her usual reaction, she was not only listening but listening intently.

"I knew there was going to be a flap this evening," she remarked when he finished. "Sophie called me this morning after you'd left for the office. She poured it all out. Odd that such a little booby should be the one to upset the apple cart, but that's often the way, isn't it? And Gilbert's more under her thumb than yours. And your mother will always side with the majority. Well, that leaves you with one thing to do, doesn't it?"

"And that is?"

"The merger, or course. The merger with United Metals."

"Oh, Katrina!" he groaned.

"I know, my dear, how painful it will be for you to lose control of a business that has been your life's work. But face it. You've already lost control."

He shook his head in misery. Katrina was life; she was market; she was truth. She knew that the merger, astutely handled—and who could handle it better than he?—would make them even richer. Nothing else really mattered to her, and she had never pretended that it did. His life was over.

The right solution didn't take long; right solutions rarely do. Harry Welles, president of United Metals, only once touched significantly on the vital issue in the merger talks, and that was when he was lunching alone with Gary in a private dining room in his office suite to arrange the latter's "golden parachute." In truth, it was more like a platinum one.

"Of course, you know, Gary, that one of the things we've most coveted in your company is yourself. I make no secret of it. We expect to call on your expertise in labor management in all of our new third world plants."

"And you're aware of my family's attitude about *that.*"

"Well aware. That's why we've made it clear in all our talks with the Kimballs that our policies abroad will undergo a drastic reassessment."

"And after the reassessment?"

Was it a nervous twitch of Welles's eyelid or a wink? "I believe the French have an expression: the more it changes, the more it's the same thing?"

Two years after the merger, when Nick Gilder ruefully decided that there had been no basic change in hiring policies abroad, he advised his wife and mother-in-law to sell out what was only a small minority position in the united companies. Gilbert had already done so, to retire to his ranch in Wyoming. The Kimballs almost doubled their investment, and Adelaide has recently bought a magnificent Lancret and Nick a new yacht. But Gary, holding on to his investment, has outdone them all. None of them, however, will speak to him. He is alone at last with Katrina.

The Scarlet Letters

IN THE midsummer of 1947 the coastal village of Glenville on the opulent north shore of Long Island was shaken by scandal. At least its principal citizens were so affected: summer and weekend residents, commuters to the big city and proprietors of the larger stores. It was not to be expected that the smaller folk would be much affected by adultery in the family of Arnold Dillard, distinguished counsel though he was to many great corporations and managing partner of the Wall Street law firm of Dillard, Kaye & Devens, known popularly as Dillard Kaye or simply Dillard K. But when the adulterer was none other than Rodman Jessup, not only the son-in-law and junior partner of Dillard but his special favorite and all-but-designated successor, a young man universally admired in the neighborhood for his impeccable morals and high ideals, and when his partner in crime, Mrs. Lila Fisk, was a middle-aged Manhattan society woman of fading charms and loose behavior, the effect on the good burghers of Glenville was comparable to that of the Hebrews when Delilah cut off Samson's curly locks. A champion had inexplicably fallen; they could only raise their hands and deplore the degeneracy of the times. Small wonder that the planet was menaced again with a third world war!

No one had seen a flaw in the Jessups' marriage. Lavinia, or Vinnie, the most adored by Dillard of his four daughters, had introduced her future husband to her father when he was a law student at Columbia, almost as though she were bringing him the son he had never had and was supposed to have passionately wanted. Pretty, bright, charming and amiable, now the mother of two daughters herself, Vinnie and her handsome husband were the undisputed leaders of Glenville's younger set.

Would Rod now come to his senses? Would he drop to his knees before his wronged bride and beg her forgiveness? Was not his legal career as well as his marriage at stake? But Rod showed no signs of repentance. He left his home in Glenville and his apartment in town and holed up in his club. He was seen at night spots with the elegantly clad Mrs. Fisk. They posed for their picture together at a charity ball. Indeed, he seemed intent on flaunting the affair. Next, it was heard that he had submitted his resignation to Dillard Kaye and that it had been accepted. Finally, it became known that Vinnie was suing him for divorce in New York on the grounds of adultery and that representing her in her father's firm was none other than Harry Hammersly, the young bachelor partner who had been known as Rod's best friend.

Arnold Dillard had never faced a personal emotional crisis as bewildering and upsetting as that caused by his son-in-law's unexampled conduct. He could not seem to find, in the well-stocked armory of his selected resources, the tool to deal with it. He had always secretly lauded himself on a precise understanding of what he liked to think of as his own highly individual and complex double personality. He had formulated a diagnosis of himself as a kind of Jekyll and Hyde—eliminating, of course, the darkest evil of the latter—and he had practiced the inner therapy (harmless, as he had then believed) of dramatizing himself as two brilliant but near opposite types. One, of course, was the prominent public figure, large, bony, broad-shouldered, grizzled, high-browed and expensively tweeded, with hard gray eyes that, however, could twinkle as well as rebuke, a legal scholar and philosopher as well as a deft administrator, a lofty idealist who was yet capable of a diplomatic compromise. The other was a man of concealed depressions, the victim of black moods in which he believed in nobody and nothing and would try to console himself behind the locked door of his study with a bottle of whiskey. But there was also a horrid little spy in his psyche that whispered to him that his melancholia was the finishing touch that the first man needed for a properly dramatic portrait.

And now, due no doubt to the high pitch of his resentment of the man who had betrayed his favorite daughter—and her father, too, oh, yes, himself as well—a fourth Arnold Dillard was emerging, a grotesque caricature of the horrid little whispering spy, a shrill hyena accusing the first two Dillards of playing God and Satan in their own Paradise Lost. Was he having a true nervous breakdown at long last?

He recalled with a searing clarity the image of the twenty-three-year-old Rodman Jessup who had first applied for a job at Dillard Kaye in the fall of 1935. Under the high-standing, wavy blond hair was a beautiful boyish face, the face of a fine clean youth, a kind of all-American cartoon. Yet the blue-gray eyes had a mature and rather fixed stare, and one felt that the muscular, well-shaped body under the tight white spotless summer suit would respond instantly to anything those eyes saw as needing correction.

Arnold had been half-apologetic about the exiguous salary then offered.

"That's all right, sir," was the prompt response. "I'm looking for opportunity rather than remuneration. I've had to work my way through Columbia College and Law School, so I know how to live on a shoestring. And if I may say so, sir, it was hearing you speak at law school commencement last year that made me apply here first. I liked the way you put the high role that lawyers can play in our business system."

Arnold looked at him carefully for a moment. "My daughter Lavinia is a friend of yours, I believe."

"I am honored if she so describes me, sir. But I wasn't going to mention her."

Of course, Rod was promptly hired. He had been editor-in-chief of his law journal and was clearly a "catch." And what, of course, clinched the matter was that Vinnie had confided in her father (though not in her mother, she flatteringly assured him, and certainly not in Rodman) her fixed determination to marry this young man.

Arnold had succumbed to the somewhat perverse temptation to submit this self-assured intruder into his family midst to the toughest office test, so he assigned the new recruit to the job of acting as his principal assistant in the most complicated of corporate reorganizations. Rod had been extraordinary. He toiled away, night and day, even sleeping on a couch in the law library, until he mastered every detail of the massive transaction with a clarity of mind and an organizing capability that had astonished and delighted his new boss. When the job was finished, Arnold took him out to a Lucullan dinner at the most expensive French restaurant in town, where, he was pleased to note, his guest partook freely of three famous wines without slurring a syllable.

As they sat over their cognac afterward, Arnold embarked on a more personal note. "Well, my boy, now you've had a glimpse of what a corporate law practice is all about, I daresay it strikes a young idealist like yourself as something a bit dustier than you'd expected. Even a bit grubbier. Isn't that so? You know the poem about the young Apollo, tiptoe on the verge of strife? How does it go? 'Magnificently unprepared for the long littleness of life'? Well, I suppose the 'magnificently' is something."

"But the details are nothing, sir, if the whole is good."

"You find a corporate reorganization good? You interest me."

"Isn't it part of the social machinery designed to get us out of this Depression? How can that not be good?

"Well, you might argue that in the matter we've just finished. But I'm afraid, my friend, you'll find that some reorganizations have no purpose loftier than to establish the control of one set of pirates over another."

Arnold, facing the cool responding stare of those blue-gray eyes, felt almost ashamed of himself. What was he doing now, old ham that he was, but trying to astonish a young man with the broad reach of his mind into the bottom as well as the top of a law practice?

"But those things are going to be done anyway, sir" was

Rod's sturdy reply. "And, as I see it, it's our job to make sure that they are done efficiently and legally. In a democracy, and in a free market, or as free as practicable, we have to let businessmen and capitalists to some extent work things out their own way. But as lawyers we can see that they work it out strictly within the law. It doesn't so much matter *what* they do as long as everyone can see it. Then, if laws have to be changed, the voters will know what to change."

Arnold nodded, musingly. "Which means that a lawyer doesn't really need a conscience at all?"

"Or the highest and most sensitive kind. Like yours, sir."

This had all been very gratifying, and the young man was evidently sincere, if almost too much so. It had not taken more than a few months before it was recognized by all twenty partners and sixty clerks of the firm that young Jessup had been enlisted among the small group of selected associates who worked almost exclusively for the senior partner. Within a year he became Arnold's son-in-law, and in another five he was made the youngest of his partners. A tour of naval duty in the Pacific war only added to his luster, and he and Vinnie, neighbors of her parents in town and tenants of a cottage on the latters' estate in Glenville, became as essential to Arnold's family as they were to his law practice. Even Vinnie's younger sisters adored their handsome and intriguingly serious brother-in-law and sought his approval of their boyfriends.

There were times when Arnold liked to think of himself as an aging Hadrian leaning on the sturdy shoulders of a stalwart Antinoüs, on whose total fidelity he could confidently rely to help him bear the burdens of the empire. But there were also moments when he was subject to the uncomfortable suspicion that his protégé was gaining control of his inner being and becoming as much a guide as a support. If there was the hint of a fanatic in Rod, there might also be the hint of a fanatic's strength.

When a vacancy on the Appellate Division prompted gossip that the governor might appoint Arnold to the seat, he discussed the situation candidly with Rod over lunch at the Downtown Association.

"But what would happen to the firm?" the latter expostulated in dismay.

"Oh, it would get along. Nobody's indispensable. And there's a side of me that would like the chance to philosophize a bit about the law. As judges can. I like to see our law as a continuing process. I want to trace our notions back to the old writs in common law."

"How many judges do that?"

"Well, call me Oliver Wendell Holmes, damn it all! Call me Cardozo! Can't there be anything in my life but Dillard Kaye? Must I go to my grave representing more or less flawed characters? I want a moment of truth. Shining truth!"

"But that's precisely what you have!" Rod exclaimed, almost fiercely. "You've forged this great law firm as your tool. Or, rather, as your shining sword. You say you're not indispensable to it, but I claim you are. There's not another firm in town with our unity, our ésprit de corps. Every one of your partners feels it is as much his club, his school, his church, I might almost say, as his business association."

Arnold at this chose to conclude the discussion, and, anyway, the governor didn't appoint him. But there was a kernel of truth in what Rod had said about the firm. Arnold *had* created a tight unit. Partners were always chosen from the associates, never brought in from the outside. There were no branch offices, even in Washington or Paris. Profits were divided evenly among the partners, varying only according to years of service. Arnold himself, it was true, received a considerably larger share as general manager, but only through the unanimous vote of the partnership, with him abstaining.

But really abstaining? Had he not known perfectly what they were up to? Had he not known that the firm was his? Had he not known that the biggest clients were all his, and that, however benevolent, however unchallenged, however assured of the united support of his nineteen cohorts, he was still a despot? And was his occasional restiveness not possibly evidence of a hidden fear that Rod Jessup was grooming himself for the successorship?

And, indeed, only a few months before the dreadful event of the flaunted adultery, came the one serious row in Arnold's halcyon relationship with his son-in-law.

The final settlement of the estate of a rich client of Arnold's was being held up pending the outcome of a suit brought by the widow of the caretaker of the decedent's Long Island estate for a bequest to her late husband of $50,000, which the executors had refused to pay on the grounds that both men were drowned when their fishing boat on Long Island Sound capsized and that there was no evidence that the caretaker had survived his employer.

Rod had marched into Arnold's office one morning and placed his determined features between his father-in-law and the breathtaking view of the harbor.

"Of course, trusts and estates are not my business, sir, but

I couldn't help hearing about the Martin case. It can't be true that you aren't going to pay that poor woman the legacy to her husband!"

"My dear boy," Arnold retorted a bit testily, "that is a matter for the executors, not for counsel, to decide. And even if trusts and estates are not your field, surely you must recall from your law school days that fiduciaries need pay only what the law requires them to pay."

"Of course, but surely the widow, who takes the residuary estate outright, as I understand it, can be advised to pay the legacy."

"I am not in the habit of advising my clients as to their moral duties."

"Couldn't you break your habit? Certainly in a case as flagrant as this one?"

Arnold felt a sudden constriction around his heart. "Aren't you being the least bit impertinent?"

Rod flushed. "I'm sorry, sir. I forgot myself."

"I will tell you this, my lad. If it will make things any easier for you. Mrs. Martin is a bitter woman. The autopsy showed that both men had been drinking heavily. She believes that it was the caretaker who brought the whiskey along in the boat and was responsible for the disaster."

A long pause followed, during which Rod paced the floor, evidently seeking to assess this information. At last he paused and faced Arnold. "Only one more question, sir. Do you agree with Mrs. Martin that the caretaker was responsible?"

Arnold was about to answer that he neither knew nor cared and that it was not his or his son-in-law's business to look into the matter further, but, somewhat to his own surprise, his reply was much milder. "As a matter of fact, I don't agree with her. Oliver Martin had been drinking for years, and it's much more probable that the unfortunate caretaker was told to bring the booze and almost forced to drink it with his boss."

"You won't tell Mrs. Martin that?"

"And lose the estate? For she's a mean one. Dream on!"

"What's an estate to a principle?"

Arnold was about to shout at him, to call him a madman, to tell him to get out of his office, when something in the glittering eyes of the young man stopped him. He thought of him suddenly as a Blake watercolor, naked, shining, an Apollo with raised arms and golden hair. Who was this young man, anyway? What was he?

"All right, Rod. I *will* tell her."

His son-in-law's smile was radiant. "I knew you would, sir. I never doubted it. I never doubted you."

Arnold talked to the widow Martin that evening, calling at her house at a time when he knew a cocktail would soften her jagged edges. She was nasty about the whole thing, but she agreed to pay half the legacy in a proposed settlement, and she did not fire her counsel.

It so happened that Rod left the next week for a protracted business trip, so Arnold did not have the opportunity to discuss again the Martin case with him before the explosion of the news of his brazen adultery.

So far as Arnold could recall there had never been a crisis in his life where he had been so hard put to bring the diverse elements of his wrath and consternation into any kind of coherent order. The great decisions of his life had always been made with gravity and calm. When he married, for example, he had been perfectly aware of the different motivations that had impelled him to select Eleanor Shattuck as his mate. He had weighed her modest physical attractions, her dry wit, her adequate dowry and her Boston blue blood against her diminutive stature, her biting sarcasm and her total failure to be impressed by his legal achievements. She had married him, he clearly saw and appreciated, for love alone, the constant and unarticulated love of a New England maid of ancient lineage who hadn't a romantic bone in her body. Why, then, could he not get to the root of the fury that Rod's betrayal aroused in him? Or was the answer that he *could* get to its root? His anger, he reluctantly conceded to himself, was not on behalf of his daughter or of his granddaughters or even, as he liked to think, on behalf of his firm. It was on behalf of himself alone.

Now what did this mean? Of course, he knew what it would mean to a slyly smiling, lewdly winking world. It would mean that his feeling for Rod was a homosexual obsession, and that his private image of himself as Hadrian and Rod as the beloved Antinoüs was only too exact. Yet he had never been conscious of a desire for any kind of physical intimacy with the young man; he had never even so much as patted him on the back. Of course, he had read too much not to be aware of the powers of repression that can drive such impulses even from the conscious mind, but if they are that deeply hidden, can they really be said to exist? He had preferred to see himself as an ancient Greek of the highest Socratic type whose sensual needs were satisfied by women but whose spiritual ones craved the company of idealistic younger men. He had even liked the idea, rather fancied himself in the role.

He found some consolation in talking over the problem of

how to handle Rod with the only person in the office who seemed to have all its threads in hand. Harry Hammersly was almost Rod's equal in brilliance, a seemingly confirmed bachelor and the intimate friend of both Rod and Vinnie. His tall, straight figure, square brow and black shiny hair might have suggested a formidable virility had his air not been mitigated by a self-deprecating smile, too much hearty laughter at the jokes of others and a conversational habit of self-mockery.

Arnold had consulted Harry before accepting Rod's resignation from the firm. He felt that the value of his son-in-law's legal services was too great to be dispensed with on his say-so alone. But Harry had seen no alternative.

"You know what pals Rod and I have always been, so you can imagine, sir, what pain it gives me to say what I have to say. Rod will be regarded by many, perhaps by the majority of your partners, as one who has offended you beyond the scope of real forgiveness. The spirit of unity that has been your great creation in Dillard Kaye would be shattered fatally if you kept him on. And you needn't be concerned about Rod's future. He will find another good post soon enough. No doubt with one of our rivals."

Arnold nodded slowly as he took this in. "And how do you think I should advise my afflicted daughter? I know she has a loyal friend in you, Harry."

"I am proud to hear you say it, sir. I think, of course, a divorce is necessary. Your pride and hers could hardly let you consider a reconciliation under the circumstances, even if one were offered, which seems most unlikely."

"I have to agree with that."

"And in choosing the jurisdiction in which to sue, I see no

reason to look beyond the borders of the state in which the wrong occurred."

"You mean New York? On the grounds of adultery? Do we want a scandal greater than we already have? What are you talking about, Harry?"

"I'm talking about something we can do for Rod. Something that may help to beat him back into the senses he seems temporarily to have lost. What the psychiatrists call shock treatment. Let him see in our papers his spades called spades, his paramour named, his sin defined. Why should we smooth it all over in a Reno fantasy where we ask for a decree because he failed to respond to a two-demand bid at a bridge table? We owe it to Rod, a man we have loved and respected, to show him just how low he has sunk. And maybe that will help him get back to his feet."

Arnold could hardly swallow. His throat was choked until he coughed several times and wiped his eyes. He recalled the day of the Armistice, in 1918, when he had been an army major on staff duty behind the front, safe from enemy fire, though not through any choice of his own, and the ecstasy he had felt at the thought of the beaten Boches, throwing down their arms and preparing to return to homes made hungry by the Allied blockade. The old song "We Bring the Jubilee!" had echoed in a heart full of righteous hate. Day of Wrath! Day of God!

"Well, Harry, there may be justice in what you say."

Despite his exaltation, Arnold knew he would have to discuss this with his wife, which he did that very night, after dinner, when they were having their coffee in the library. She sat there, impassive, enigmatic, on the other side of the fireplace, her black beady eyes, under her pasty brow and messy auburn hair, fixed on him as he talked. She had not attracted him physically for a decade or more; her native high spirits had faded, little by little, as if they were Boston foliage bound to wither in a New York climate.

"You seem unusually Zeus-like today, my dear," she offered at last. "When may I expect the first thunderbolt?"

He used to tell friends, more or less jocularly, that Eleanor exceeded Browning's last duchess in that her ribald laughs rather than her smiles "went everywhere," including in his direction, and that, had he been a Renaissance despot, he might have "given commands." She prided herself, he knew only too well, on her contempt for social snobbery, for "pseudo-intellectualism" and for the vanities of dress and domestic elegance, but the austerity of her absolute faith in the essential moral rightness of her Shattuck and Lowell ancestors made something of a desert of whatever bright colors and excitements Manhattan and Glenville had to offer. The air of the desert, however, was clear and dry. For if her Beacon Street ancestors had lifted her above the strife of Fifth and Park Avenue social climbers, so had her transcendental ones (she had Emerson blood as well) freed her from the clutch of religious creeds. Eleanor, on the ramparts of the Colony Club, brandished her weapons alone.

Somewhat gruffly, Arnold summarized his discussion with Hammersly.

"Harry recommends a New York divorce?" she queried. "And we thought him and Rodman such pals."

"He's thinking of Vinnie. Why should the poor child have to take herself to some godless western state and swear falsely that she resides in it, when our own legislature in Albany has provided the just and effective remedy for the wrong she has received?"

"Why? To avoid a stinking scandal; that's why."

"The scandal is already here. Our son-in-law has seen to that!"

"But you'd make it worse. And don't talk to me about false swearing. Your firm has sent plenty of clients to Reno, including your niece, who had the same grounds of complaint as Vinnie."

"That was different."

"It was different in that you had no particular resentment against her husband. You just wanted to get rid of him; that was all. And she had another fool ready to marry her."

"Which is hardly Vinnie's case."

"What do you really know about Vinnie's case? What's got you worked up is Rod. I've never seen you so violent."

"And what about you?" he demanded, raising his voice to take the offensive. "Wouldn't a little violence become a mother whose daughter has been so foully treated? But no, you must always be the priestess of the life of reason. I daresay you think Rodman is behaving only as most men would, given half a chance. Isn't that part of your blind faith in cynicism? It's a great way, I suppose, of avoiding upsetting emotions."

Eleanor cut through his reproaches to make a single point. "I don't think Rod is behaving at all like other men. He's basically a puritan. Maybe it takes a Bostonian to see that."

"Well, he's certainly not acting like a puritan."

"But maybe he's reacting like one. A puritan turned inside out."

"A puritan gone to the devil, you mean?"

"That could be it. Maybe he hasn't learned that if God is dead, the devil must be, too."

"Which is taking us a long way from choosing a forum for the divorce."

"Oh, if you're going to get it, I don't really care where. And I suppose the divorce is inevitable. You don't hear much these days of reconciliations. The first thing that goes wrong in a marriage, and, bang, call the lawyer. And after that it's hopeless."

"The bar has always had your good opinion, my dear."

It had been easy to predict that Eleanor's reaction to the proposed method of divorce would irritate him, but Vinnie's came as a surprise to her father. She seemed upset, nervous, fidgety, during their conference in his office, where they met to emphasize the gravity of what he proposed. Twice she rose and strode to the window to contemplate the view. He thought she looked less pretty than usual, and he hated this, for her looks were always important to him. The big blond girl with the laughing blue eyes and cheerful smile had become plumper with the years, not enough to make her in the least unattractive but enough to take her out of the category of beauties in which he had once so proudly placed her. Arnold could not understand why his motherly old secretary, Mrs. Peck, insisted that her added pounds had made her rounder and "sexier."

She uttered a little cry of dismay when he came to the point about the New York divorce.

"You side with Harry, then?"

"I most certainly do."

"Well, if both of you agree, what can I do but go along? I know Mummy's against it, but then Mummy's always basically neutral, and she doesn't really care. I've been brought up all my life to think of Dillard Kaye as something that couldn't be wrong. As a kind of holy tribunal. Or King Arthur's round table. Where all the knights were perfect gentlemen and invincible fighters. And Rod as Lancelot. And now look what's happening. Lancelot is being thrown out of Camelot!"

"Not for an affair with King Arthur's wife!" Arnold couldn't help interjecting.

"Not with Mummy, hardly!" Here Vinnie broke into a kind of gasping laughter that shocked her father. Had she been drinking? At ten o'clock in the morning? "No, he's more like Satan than Lancelot, isn't he? So he must be cast out of heaven, down, down, down ..." She leaned over and stared at the floor.

"So there we are, my dear," Arnold murmured in a softer tone, beginning to be alarmed at her uncharacteristic mood.

"Well, I guess I must do as I'm told, Daddy. One rebellion in Dillard Kaye is surely enough for one year."

"Vinnie! You're beginning to sound like your mother."

Her father, at least until her marriage, and arguably even afterward, had been the principal figure in Vinnie's life, and she presumably in his. He had made little secret of his preference for his oldest, prettiest and brightest daughter over the other three, which the latter had accepted, almost without jealousy, as a fact of life, evident from their earliest days and also as a matter not of the first importance. The overworked and constantly absent American father of the nineteen twenties and thirties was not the primary figure of the home, and the younger Dillards turned for the permission needed for their various pleasures to the actual ruler of the household, Mummy. And Eleanor Dillard tended to regard her eldest daughter's total dependence on her father as something of a welcome relief, as if the latter were reducing her parental burdens from four to three. Which did not keep her, however, from being sarcastic about their relationship, describing it to her cronies as a Victorian pastel of the benevolent aging sire stroking the golden hair of the lovely child whose eyes are fixed adoringly on his. Couldn't one see it as the ultimately idealized union of the sexes, with the male providing wisdom and strength and loving protection while the female furnished an absolute loyalty and a purity of body and mind? Union of the sexes? No! Abolition of sex! Wasn't that what a true civilization required?

Vinnie had never quite understood her mother, but she deplored her detachment and feared her tart tongue. She saw how some other girls controlled their mothers by turning down or off the daily show of affection the latter seemed to need, but her mother did not appear to have any such necessity. Her father, of course, was just the opposite, at least where she was concerned, and she did not hesitate to draw heavily on the large balance of love that he kept in store for her. She had love to return to him, indeed, but her love went hand in hand with a shrewd habit of appraisal that did not characterize his—in her case, at any rate. Thus, she had quite understood that when he had offered her the alternative of a splendid debutante party, with all the trimmings, or a trip to Europe with a girlfriend, she would get both if she chose the latter, so she did. And when he promised her a large check if she didn't smoke or drink hard liquor until she was twenty-one, she agreed, knowing that she could plead with him successfully for dispensations for certain weekends and holidays. But she also deeply appreciated the vast scope of his mind and outreaches—she deemed him to know everything from Anglo-Saxon law to Dadaism—and she conceived of it as a sacred duty—made more sacred by her mother's patent neglect of it—to be an acolyte at his altar. An acolyte, of course, could rise, could be a cardinal to a pope or an éminence grise to a king, couldn't he? And one of her greatest contributions would be to bring her father, by way of a son-in-law, the son he had always wanted.

She met Rodman Jessup at a party given for her in Glenville by her parents on her twenty-first birthday, when her father handed her, along with the apparently hard-earned martini, the large promised check. Rodman was the houseguest of Dillard neighbors, and Vinnie, instantly impressed by his good looks and serious, assured manner, had slipped into the dining room during the cocktail hour to change the place cards so that he would be next to her. He seemed to drop into her life like a prince in a fairy tale.

He was, however, no prince. His father had died in the war and he had been raised, an only child, by a widowed and desolate mother who had supplemented a small income with the offerings of better-off relatives. For the Jessups, like many large Manhattan clans, had connections among the rich as well as the middle class. Rodman had fulfilled all of his devoted mother's hopes, as well as the more sober expectations of the contributing kin, by graduating *summa cum laude* from Columbia College and becoming the editor of the law journal. And as luck would have it, he was already a strong admirer of Arnold Dillard.

There was little coyness between him and Vinnie. They expressed almost at once their mutual attraction and were soon going out together in town on the few nights when he was not working. She had finished at Vassar and was unemployed, and she had no desire to embark on any work until she decided how this new friend was going to change her life. For all the gravity of his airs and thoughts, he was capable of bursts of enthusiasm and excitability, which she found utterly charming. He talked, it was true, a great deal about himself. But that was because there was a world before him that he could hardly wait to conquer.

"Of course, you're going to apply to Dillard Kaye for a job," she told him one night at the automat where he took her for supper. She liked the fact that he never apologized for, or even mentioned, his limitation to inexpensive spots. It showed that he took for granted that she was above such things.

"You think they'd take me?" he inquired earnestly. "I'm hardly a white shoe type. I didn't even go to a prep school. And I'm told most of the partners are in the *Social Register.*"

"That's because most of them have worked their way up. Daddy doesn't give a hoot about those distinctions. I thought you knew that."

"Oh, I wasn't thinking of *him.* To work for him would be my dream of dreams!"

"Please! You'll be making me think I'm only a rung in your ladder to fame."

He became instantly solemn. "You couldn't think anything as awful as that, could you, Vinnie?"

"Why not? A talented young man without a fortune has to look about him to get started. In Europe it's taken quite for granted that one of the functions of a wife is to have something to give a push to a climber, whether it be blood or connections or just hard cash."

"Vinnie, I don't want you to talk that way. Those things have nothing to do with you and me. Tell me that you believe that, Vinnie. Tell me, please."

She was a bit taken aback by his gravity, but she decided to take it as a compliment. "Of course, I was only joking."

She discovered that his stern morality was absolutely consistent. He had no use for ambiguities or double standards. When she told him of a Vassar classmate who, finding herself pregnant at the termination of a wholly clandestine love affair, had availed herself of an abortion, without telling her family, he was shocked. She should have had the child, he argued.

"But it would have been her social ruin," Vinnie protested. "She wanted to go on with her life as before. The way her lover was doing. Of course, no one would have much blamed him, even if it had become known."

"*I* would have blamed him. Just as much as I blame her. Even more, perhaps, because as a man he should have been stronger against temptation."

Vinnie decided that she might as well have this out with him, there and then. "You hold that a man should keep himself as pure as a woman?"

"Why should he have any lesser obligation?"

"And that he should be a virgin until he marries?"

"If he expects it of her, why not of himself?"

"But what about the old theory that he should have enough experience to initiate his bride in the rites of love?"

"Does it take so much experience? The birds and the bees don't seem to think so."

"They haven't been petrified by civilization. They haven't had to wear clothes."

"You think Adam and Eve had an easier time? Well, of course, he had no choice, for she was the only woman. I don't think that you'll find me lacking in that respect if you marry me."

"Heavens!" she gasped. "Is this a proposal?"

"It would be, if there were any chance of its being accepted."

"Too soon, too soon," she murmured, almost breathless at his precipitancy. When he wasn't too serious, he was almost too light. But there was no mistaking the yank at her heart. She had brought this man into her life, and she was going to have to cope with him. "I need more time, my friend. Only don't think I'm letting you off the hook. I shall remember that you have made a formal proposal."

"It's not binding, of course, until accepted. And it must be accepted within a reasonable time. How long shall we give it?"

"Say a year?"

But it took only six months. They were married immediately after his graduation from law school, and had the summer to themselves before he started to work at Dillard Kaye.

Vinnie came in time to reflect that too much good fortune may turn into a cloying feast. One of her Vassar classmates had married a handsome Jewish boy who had helped her to her feet after a bad tumble on a Central Park skating rink. Her family shared the routine social anti-Semitism of the New York society of that day, and his family was devoutly Orthodox. Spurned by all four parents, the young couple had eloped in a frenzy of romantic delight and were forgiven by both families on the birth of the first baby. Vinnie ruefully contrasted the excitement of their Romeo and Juliet story with the heavy blanket of congratulation that had almost stifled the pleasure of her engagement.

Had she immolated herself, an Iphigenia, on the altar of her father's ideals? In bringing him the son he craved, had she lost her own position in his life?

Yet her marriage proved to be just what she thought she wanted. Rod worked joyfully and serenely with her father and attained not only an early partnership in the firm but achieved the undisputed position of right hand to the man whom everyone referred to as the "chief." She and Rod, in town and in country, lived in close proximity to the Dillards; indeed, the two households made up what was distinctly the first family of Glenville. Two little girls, in perfect health, were born to Vinnie and Rod, the product of his regular and spirited, if always predictable love-making. And she had taken an active part in local charities and had become the admired chairman of the board of the Manhattan day school that her daughters attended.

But if she had achieved in life exactly what she intended, she had also the bitterness of recognizing the Greek origin of those bearing her gifts. As a heaven without end can become at first cloying and at last fraught with terror, she began to look about her with bewildered eyes. When her father and husband, after a hearty Sunday lunch, reverted to an animated discussion of their last corporate reorganization, she would sometimes wonder whether their Garden of Eden, which she had helped to plant and water, was really open to either Eves or snakes. And when Rod insisted that she was the radiant guide and influence of his life, she had the nasty suspicion that what he really meant was the stimulus he received from their weekly coitus. It may have been for him a kind of beneficial physical exercise.

There was plenty of antidote, it was true, to the paternal and spousal idealism in her mother's freely expressed cynicism, but she had always discounted this as the self-compensation of a sour old woman for her inability to express her love, or her lack of love, to her husband and family.

Where help came to her, if help it was, was from Harry Hammersly. Harry and Rod seemed to represent the attraction of opposites. Best friends in college and law school and now law partners, they always remained in constant touch with each other. Yet Harry, a merry bachelor, was as mocking and impudent and charming as his friend was sober, polite and at times a bit grim. And if he made fun of the world, he made particular fun of Rod. Rod, however, did not appear to mind it. Like a fool in a medieval court, Harry was licensed, at least in Rod's domain, to say what he liked.

Vinnie had originally supposed that she would disapprove of Harry. His impudence verged on heresy, and he laughed at too many sacred things. But his apparent assumption that her wit and wide views lifted her to his level of isolated liberty, making them lonely partners in a world of amiable philistines whom it was their duty to entertain, was flattering. And his well-made, soft, very white-skinned body, which she had once found faintly repellent, even effeminate, she was bothered to find increasingly intriguing to her. The sensuous way he twisted his torso, particularly after making an off-color joke, she reluctantly admitted, titillated her. And in his rare moments of repose, as when he was listening to her—and a very attentive listener he could be—his handsome Roman face waxed almost noble, though he soon enough shattered the impression with his high, almost screeching laugh, as though otherwise some deed of heroism might be horridly expected of him.

At length she began to suspect that there was something subtly undermining in the persistence of his jokes at her husband's expense. And that there might be something disturbing in her own acceptance of these.

One Sunday afternoon in Glenville, when the three of them were seated on the terrace by her father's tennis court after a game of singles between Rod and Harry, which Rod had finally won, the conversation fell on the trial of a famous gangster who was, surprisingly, being represented by a respectable law firm. Vinnie asked whether Dillard Kaye would have taken such a case, and Rod firmly denied it.

"But doesn't even the most hardened criminal deserve a good defense?" she asked.

"Certainly, and hardened criminals can be very picky in choosing counsel, particularly if they're rich. The problem, however, would not arise for us. No gangster would ever come knocking at *our* door. He'd know that his defense would be an absolutely honest one, with no dirty tricks. And that's the last thing they want."

"You imply that the firm representing this gangster is using dirty tricks?"

"If it deems them necessary, yes. We're not all perfect."

"Only Dillard Kaye?"

"Only Dillard Kaye." Rod smiled to make the boast a jest, but what he felt was clear enough.

"I wonder," Harry now observed, "if we would be quite so pure if we didn't have a plethora of less tainted fees. We can afford to dispense with dirty tricks. At least with the dirty tricks of the mob."

"You mean you have other kinds?" Vinnie demanded.

"Oh, we have our nuances and our innuendoes." But here he raised his voice to make another point and distract Rod from what threatened to be a hearty rebuttal. "So you see, my dear Vinnie, how Rod maneuvers to avoid the embarrassment of turning down a would-be client in trouble. He presents the unclean creature with an array of virtues like flashlights pointed at the hiding places of guilt!"

Seated beside Harry a week later at one of her father's Sunday lunches, she decided to get a few things straight. In the mock serious tone one adopts when one is really serious, she asked him, "You don't believe in anything, do you, Harry? I mean in God or ethical principles or anything like that?"

"Well, I'm a positivist, if that's what you mean. It all has to be proved to me. I believe in taste. Good taste and bad."

"You mean like in decorating?"

"If you like. That's one aspect of it. I think it's good taste not to rob or murder or covet your neighbor's wife." Here he rolled his eyes comically. "Though I might be forgiven the last."

She did not comment on this. "And you certainly don't find it good taste to laud the sanctity of Dillard Kaye."

"I don't find my partners apostles, as some do; no."

"You mean Rod."

"Well, he seems to find your father one."

"And you don't."

Harry laughed. "Oh, I admire him! He can thunder like Jehovah and grin like Satan. He's a primordial demiurge."

"I think Rod really worships him."

"Oh, Rod approaches him as the monkeys approach the rock python Kaa in *The Jungle Book*. But one day he'll come too close and get caught in those writhing coils."

"What do you mean by that?"

"You'll see, my dear. You'll see." And he ended the discussion by turning, with the roast, to his other neighbor.

Harry didn't work as many nights in the office as Rod did, claiming that if one arrived at eight in the morning and stayed until seven at night and didn't "shoot the breeze" with fellow workers and take a two-hour lunch, one could get one's work done. The result was that he was often free to take Vinnie to plays or concerts to which she had tickets but to which, at the last moment, her husband could not go. And sometimes he would take her afterward for a nightcap to his elegant little penthouse, with its sweeping view north of the great green oblong of Central Park.

Listening to him as he took apart the world of her Lares and Penates—indeed, pleasantly accustomed to it as she was growing—it somehow proved to her that all her repressed doubts and reservations had not been merely the idle fancies that flutter through any mind, but were substantial parts of herself, and sins as well, real sins. What made her almost welcome the recognition of sin was that it had a reality that her previous recognitions, or fancied recognitions, had lacked. She might be damned, but didn't one have to have been alive before one was damned? Wasn't it possibly worth it?

As her talks with Harry became more and more personal,

he told her about the problems of his private life. He had, the year before, broken off a long affair with a woman because she wanted to marry him.

"But why didn't you marry her?" Vinnie had asked.

"Because I didn't love her."

"But, Harry, the time may have come when you ought to settle down. You're not twenty-one, my dear. Some men are not destined to fall head over heels in love. I don't think the greatest men are apt to feel passion in that way. Daddy, for example. He's never really loved my mother. But you want to have a family and children, don't you?"

"With the right woman, yes."

"And what sort of woman is that?"

"Well, say a woman like you."

She did not reply to this, and he didn't press the point. But they continued, on other occasions, to discuss sexual problems with what she liked to think was a clinical detachment, and in due course they came to an analysis of hers. Harry at last extracted from her the admission that she had never had sex with any man but Rod.

"I think it's a pity," he informed her, "for any woman to be so limited. I'm not saying anything about Rod's performance in bed, which I'm sure is very fine, but there are joys in variety and experimentation, and in an ideal society no one, man or woman, should be confined for life to a single mate. There should be ways of extending one's experience without incurring blame for broken vows. Indeed, that is why wife-swapping is a not uncommon suburban practice."

"Really? Do you think it ever happens in Glenville?"

"I know damn well it happens in Glenville."

"Rod would die at the very idea."

"I agree that he would. So it could never happen to him. Anyway, I have no wife to offer him in return."

"And just what the hell do you mean by *that?*"

"My dear Vinnie, you know very well what I mean by that."

Which, of course, she did. Which, of course, they had been leading each other on to. And indeed she did find feverishly rewarding the different ways of love-making to which her highly imaginative and widely experienced guide introduced her. In this new school she proved herself an eager and proficient student, and the guilt that now assailed her in every hour when she was not with Harry seemed only to add to the intensity of her pleasure. When she thought of the horror that some of her doings would arouse in Rod and in her father, when she heard ringing in her head their exclamations of "decadent" and "depraved," she thought, with an acceptance and resignation that brought some relief, that heaven and hell had to be different places and never the twain would meet.

Toward Harry she now felt a dependence that was more like the blind devotion of a dog than a love in any romantic sense of the word. She took him as a kind of new god who had raped her and become her master. She did not mind the suspicion, rapidly growing to a conviction, that she figured in his plans for ultimate promotion in the firm, though she did not exactly see how, and she also, but without resentment, made out that he must for years have been jealous of Rod's heroic reputation as a Galahad of noble life and sought in the debauching of his wife a revenge for his own moral inferiority.

One Sunday morning, when Rod was away on a business

trip, and she had gone to Harry's flat instead of taking the girls to church, and she found herself nude, kneeling down on his living room rug before his standing nude figure, her hands clasping his buttocks and her lips receiving his ejaculated sperm, she knew, with a dreary satisfaction, that she had no further to fall.

◇

On a morning when Rod had an uptown appointment, he decided after lunch not to go back to his office, but to spend the afternoon working in his apartment. The girls would be at school until five; Vinnie had gone to Glenville for the day; so it would be quiet. He kept certain of his files in a closet that was also used as his liquor cabinet, and it was usually locked, as their cleaning woman was not above the temptation of an occasional nip. He had different hiding places for the key, and he now remembered that he had slipped it into one of the drawers of his wife's dressing table under a pile of her underwear. Reaching for it, his hand struck a notebook. Flipping the pages in surprise, he saw it was full of Vinnie's handwriting, and when he made out one sentence, he sat heavily down, ice sliding over his heart like a glacier, and read the journal through.

Vinnie had faithfully recorded what she and Harry had done. The journal was an inventory of acts. What had induced her to record it? Some remnant of conscience, some throwback to her mother's puritan ancestry? For a wild moment he thought it might be fiction. But it was too graphic. For another moment his curiosity was so keen that he could almost set aside the scarlet fact that his world was in tiny pieces, scattered all over the room. But when he rose at last to his feet, he tottered and almost fell. Then he returned the journal to its place and closed the drawer. He left the apartment and walked to Central Park, where he sat for two hours on a bench.

What he began to realize, slowly, but with a creeping ineluctability, was that this experience, which was like nothing that had happened to him before, seemed to be occurring to a person other than himself, a new man, perhaps even an opposite. For what sort of man would have married a woman capable of doing what Vinnie had described on the last page of her abominably honest journal? Or did all women do it, or want to do it, and had he been living in a paradise of idiotic fools? Was it even conceivable that he could want a woman to do it to *him?* Was *that* why the horrid journal had an eerie fascination for him, over and above the wrath and indignation it inspired? Or should have inspired? How could he know what might or might not arouse the lust of the new man that Rod Jessup had become in a single morning?

He then walked rapidly twice around the reservoir, only to find that his head was aching and that there was a queer buzzing in his ears. He sat again on a bench until this passed away. It broke upon him suddenly that the person who had to be protected from all this horror was his father-in-law. Arnold Dillard must never have an inkling of what his daughter and Harry were up to. The disillusionment might otherwise cause Dillard to lose faith in what his whole life had stood for. The copulations—and other things—of which the lecherous couple had been guilty should be sealed up forever in their marriage, Harry's marriage to the boss's daughter, which, Rod was sure, had been Harry's motive from the beginning. And that marriage could take place only if Rod himself were removed from the picture with Arnold's full approval. And there was only one sure way to bring that about.

He called his secretary from a booth and told her to tell his wife that he had to go out of town on business. Then he called Lila Fisk. Was she free to dine with him at the Colony Restaurant? She was surprised, but she was free, and a few hours later he faced her across a corner table at the costliest eatery in town, raising his cocktail glass to click it against hers in a silent toast.

Lila Fisk, raven-haired, alabaster pale, with a conspiratorial smile, rich and richly attired in black satin with large pearls, was a plump but still radiant forty. She was also a hearty and genial divorcée who had been wed three times and had apparently retired from the matrimonial market to live entirely for pleasure. She was a great pal of Harry Hammersly, through whom she had come to know the Jessups. Vinnie, who was not usually partial to epicurean types, had recently taken to her. It was not hard for Rod now to understand why. He also understood that Lila had been for some time attracted to him. A virtuous man was always a challenge to her.

"Are you having a row with Vinnie?" she demanded.

"Why do you ask?"

"You're not a man to ask a lady out without your wife unless you have a point to make. You want to get back at her for something."

"It couldn't be because the man finds himself greatly attracted to the lady?"

"Oh, it could be. But then he'd take her to a less conspicuous spot. There's Arlina, from the *Sun Times*, who's already taken us in."

"Do you care?"

"I don't give a damn. But I want you to know what I know.

And now let's not spoil our evening with too many questions."

They talked, merrily enough, on other topics—she was an omnivorous reader, an avid theater-goer and a baseball fan—and after their dinner they went to her handsome Park Avenue apartment, where they had several drinks and made love. He was pleasantly surprised to find it not only simple but exhilarating. Yet she wouldn't let him spend the night; she kicked him out at midnight, with the injunction: "If you want to make it up with Vinnie now, you'll find it easier. Your guilt will cool your anger."

How much did she know about Vinnie and Harry? He was not to find out, but at any rate he had no idea of "making it up" with Vinnie. Lila agreed to dine out with him twice more, including a visit to a nightclub, where they were photographed together, but when he suggested that he move from his club into her apartment, she was profoundly shocked.

"Are you out of your mind? No one objects to an affair, if it's carried on with some discretion, but women my age don't *live* with men. Not in society. Not yet. Are you trying to ruin what shred of reputation I have left?"

"What's wrong with our living together?"

"What's wrong? What's right? Do you want to drive Vinnie into divorcing you for adultery? My God, man, maybe that's just what you *do* want! You're a lunatic, Rodman Jessup! Go home to your club, or wherever you hang out, and don't come near me again until you've learned to act like a gentleman!"

The strange thing about the next three months was that not once, even through the divorce proceedings and the negotiations following his resignation from the firm, did he have a word of direct communication with his wife or her father or Harry Hammersly.

The divorce decree awarded custody of his two daughters to Vinnie, but he had weekend and summer visitation rights. And she did not claim a penny of alimony. In two months' time he read of her marriage to her lover. He had won!

The next five years were to bring fame and fortune to Rodman Jessup. He had hardly settled himself in a new apartment, and adjusted himself to the life of a divorced parent who took his daughters to the movies on Saturday afternoons, when he was invited to lunch by an old law school classmate, Newbold Armstrong, in a newly formed club atop a skyscraper in midtown, whither much of the Wall and Broad Street legal and financial community was already beginning to move. Armstrong, the handsome, clean-cut scion of an old New York clan, was a partner in a new and aggressive law firm that was making a notorious name for itself in the burgeoning field of amalgamating different businesses into conglomerates. After one cocktail and a brief and perfunctory inquiry into his old friend's health and family, Armstrong came right to the point. Would Rod consider a partnership in his firm?

Rod restrained the impulse to wrinkle his nose. "I'm not a great fan of the take-over business. Some of it strikes me as verging on dirty pool. I'm sorry to say that, Newbold, but you and I may as well be frank with each other. At Dillard Kaye we used to turn down those retainers."

"Dillard Kaye is beginning to show its age, my friend. And you'll soon enough see the truth of that. Survival in these days depends on keeping up with the times. Luckily for me, the Armstrongs always made a point of that. One of my grandfathers acted as a broker for 'Uncle' Dan Drew, the greatest rascal on Wall Street. And a great-aunt of mine married a son of Jay Gould, whom no respectable family would let into their house by the front door. And look at us now! We're doing fine, thank you. I had rather hoped, Rod, that the way you'd been treated by your old firm and family-in-law, for doing something three quarters of the men I know have done at one point or another in their lives, would have opened your eyes. Of course, I have to admit that you weren't very tactful in the way you behaved. But that was probably because you'd always been such a Christer. You hadn't learned that it's not what you do that counts. It's how you do it."

Rod fixed a long silent stare on his luncheon host. "You know, Newbold, there may be something in what you say."

"There's a hell of a lot in what I say."

"Won't it create bitterness among the associates in your firm if you take in a partner from outside ahead of them?"

"Oh, I daresay they won't like it. But they're used to it. Everyone 'buys' partners from the outside these days. The only man who'll really mind is the partner we'll be dumping if we get hold of you."

"Why he? What's he done?"

"His billings don't add up, Rod. The days are gone when a firm will keep on some old geezer who's ceased to produce. We're not a retirement home, after all. I'll bet that at Dillard Kaye you've got some old farts who've been eating free off you for years."

Rod nodded grimly. "Probably. And of course the same thing would happen to me in your firm if I didn't pan out."

"And to me, too!" Newbold cheerfully agreed. "But I'm betting on us. Who wants special treatment? Come to us, Rod, and I'll count on you to become our star man in gobbling up vulnerable companies."

"What makes you think I'd be so good at that?"

His friend chose to make a joke of it. His laugh was loud and free. "Because you've taken off the mask, buddy. You're not Little Red Riding-hood's granny anymore. You're the big bad wolf!"

Rod took the job, and in two years' time he was generally considered one of the ablest take-over lawyers in the city. He married his secretary, a dazzling blonde of twenty-five who was as smart as she was efficient and who had the grace to maintain the hero worship for her handsome and successful boss when she graduated from amanuensis to wife. And it hardly surprised him when Harry Hammersly telephoned to suggest that they let bygones be bygones and meet for lunch.

Harry's manner, as closely observed by his former partner across the table, was as easy as ever. He didn't manifest any of the embarrassment that even such a sophisticate as he must have felt. Rod was gratified to note that when he recalled the acts that Harry and his former wife had performed together, as recorded in her infamous journal, he experienced no anger and little disgust. He had moved decisively into a different world.

Harry did not beat around the bush any more than Newbold Armstrong had two years earlier. He wanted Rod to come back to Dillard Kaye at double the pay he was now receiving. As to his position in the old partnership, he could write his own ticket. Harry made it clear that they needed him badly, not only to set up a conglomerate department but to revise the management of the badly stumbling firm. Rod was impressed by Harry's cleverness in realizing that a blunt statement of the facts was the best way to handle the man he had so deeply wronged. Harry had the genius to see that what Rod wanted above anything else was to triumph over the world that Rod himself had maneuvered into excluding him.

"But what about Arnold? How will he feel about taking back his ex-son-in-law?"

"Arnold will not be a problem, Rod. Arnold is not the man he was. He had a stroke a month ago, and though he's recovered his speech and pretty much the use of his arms and legs, he's a shadow of the old Arnold. I've discussed you with him, and he's taken it all like a lamb, just shaking his head."

"He still comes into the office?"

"Yes, but only from habit and to look at his mail. He does no work of significance. I even showed him that nasty cartoon of you in that rag *The Unconfidential Clerk*, and he only shrugged his shoulders."

"Why did you show him that?" The periodical in question, hated by the big law firms, purported to show their clerks exactly how their employers operated. The cartoon depicted Rod on his knees by an overturned garbage pail, ransacking its contents for dirt on some company a client of his was seeking to harass into submission.

"Because if that rag has it in for you, it means you're the hottest thing in take-overs!"

Less than half a year later, Rod was installed in the largest private office of the firm now named Dillard, Hammersly and Jessup, at the end of a corridor containing the adjoining offices of the two partners and four associates, all brilliant takeover experts, whom he had induced to sever their ties with Armstrong and join him in his new affiliation. His old friend and former partner, Newbold, had wildly threatened to sue him, but everyone knew it was an idle threat, and Rod had thrown back at him his own words on the importance of keeping up with the times.

Arnold, poor broken old man, had greeted him joyously, as if no cloud had ever darkened their covering sky. Though confined to a wheelchair, he loved to come to the office and lunch with any of the partners whom Harry Hammersly could induce to spare the time. He took to wheeling himself into Rod's office to chat, and the latter's time he so wasted became something of a problem. Rod decided at last that he had better drop a hint to his former mother-in-law.

He had his chance to do this one day when he heard that Eleanor Dillard was coming to the office to sign a new will. Meeting her in the reception hall, he invited her to lunch with him at his club, and she accepted, giving him what he took to be a rather forbidding smile. She was smaller, older, dryer, with even scantier hair, but her nose and eyes were as sharp as ever.

"It will be like old times," she said, enigmatically.

But it wasn't. Before he had a chance to introduce his rather awkward subject, she drove it from his mind altogether with a startling comment.

"I should tell you right off, Rod, that I always knew why you did what you did with Mrs. Fisk. You knew all about Vinnie and Harry, didn't you?"

"How in God's name did you know that?"

"It was the only thing that made it all add up."

"And did you tell Vinnie or Harry? Did you tell your husband?"

"I didn't tell a soul. I didn't see that it was any of their business. They had their own principles or life styles or what have you. They could work it out for themselves."

"And have they? Have Vinnie and Harry?"

"I think so. In their own way. He's the acting head of the firm, or will be unless you replace him. Which was what he was always after and which he'd never have been had you stayed on. And Vinnie has finally faced—what she must have always suspected—that she had been thoroughly used. Now, she's much less subservient. She knows that if he doesn't give her everything she wants, she can do him a lot of damage. Arnold isn't what he was by any means, but he still carries weight with the older partners and major clients. And Harry knows that. He's no fool. Besides, he still has something of a physical hold over Vinnie. She's a passionate woman, that child of mine, and she hasn't got any prettier with increased avoirdupois. Wait till you see her, which I gather you haven't yet. If she had to get another man today, I'm afraid she'd have to buy one."

Rod was shocked by such detachment. "I take it you're not much drawn to your son-in-law."

"Drawn to him? I detest him."

"Is he aware of that?"

"Probably. As I say, he's no fool. But he's not afraid I'll do anything to harm him. He's smart enough to know that people like me, who have no reserves in their thinking, are the opposite in their acting. They don't care to rock boats. Perhaps it's because truth is enough for them without trying to establish it. Or is it that they see how often action is futile? If they know thought is all, they may also know it's not much."

Rod sighed at such bleakness. Did she have a heart? But, then, did he? Did either of them need one anymore?

"May I ask you, Mrs. Dillard, what you think of my being back in the firm? And the way it's going now?"

"The way it's going?"

"Well, you know your husband always used to turn up his nose at the take-over business. He said it was shyster stuff. Using the courts to bedevil an opponent rather than to gain a sum due or to prevent an injustice. A kind of blackmail, he called it. Give me control or I'll ruin you."

"Well, it never seemed to me that some of the corporate practices that went on in the past were all that different. A lot of those practices have been outlawed, so now you boys have to try to gain the same ends legally. I think that even Arnold, who used to find the practice of law so uplifting, has had his doubts about it, at least since Harry took your place in his life. Or tried to take it."

"You think then that it's all a matter of there being less hypocrisy today?"

"There's certainly less of it. Indeed, I wonder at times if there's any of it left. And I must admit I miss it. Justice Holmes said once that the sight of heroism bred a faith in heroism. And I don't see much heroism in the world about me."

"Are you losing your faith in it? Harry used to tell me he believed in no absolute moral rules. That there was only taste, and that good taste was what kept him from crimes like murder and robbery."

Eleanor appeared to be little impressed by Harry's values. "I have the good taste, anyway, to reject Harry. And to prefer the old Rod Jessup to the new."

"And what was the old Rod Jessup?"

"A proud, stiff, idealistic puritan right out of the pages of Hawthorne!"

"And an anachronism."

"But such a pretty one. Leave me my memories; they're all I've got." She turned to the menu. "Let's not be too serious, Rod. I think I'm going to content myself with a salad. If taste is all we have left, I trust it will be a good one."

Rod followed her lead and picked up the card. But he was quite resolved not to bring up the subject of Arnold's inopportune visits to his office. There would at least be that much left of the "old" Rod Jessup.